LICHII BA'CHO

D JORDAN REDHAWK

Bella

Acknowledgments

Wow, who to thank? With this book it's a tough question. *Lichii Ba'Cho* has been decades in the making with a multitude of inspirational people and ideas.

In the beginning, there was…*Cyberpunk*. The role-playing game, not the genre. And with that came the character, Drill, leader of Tribe Redhawk—an American Indian family-oriented motorcycle gang. (Yes, to all those who have wondered, I legally took the name of not only a fictional character, but one of my own creation. It's a cool name!) Which means I have to mention my wife, Anna, and my gaming friends at the time—Lynn, D.T., Adrian, Jay, and Sean. They were present at the inception of *Lichii Ba'Cho*.

Next would be the readers and writers of the Xenaverse alternative fanfiction websites. This story was originally posted in 1998, and a lot of people kept wanting more. I received many emails stating how much this tale resonated with everyone despite the fact that I considered it one of my worst written novellas. (Author ducks behind computer screen to avoid rotten tomatoes thrown at her.) Barbara MacClay and Miguel even created artwork for the thing. (Good stuff, too!) Thanks to both of you as well as everyone else who wrote begging for the next installment until it was completed.

This current version sees additional thank-you's—Anna Redhawk, Shawn Cady and Anita Pawlowski, my first readers. Always there, always with questions, always supporting me. You guys are the best! Nancy Ashmore, editor extraordinaire, who I met back in the Xenaverse days. She's been a major influence with my dangling participles ever since. (Hey! Get your mind outta the gutter!) Thanks for sticking through life with me, Nancy, not only as an editor but as a dear friend!

And Bella Books, of course! I haven't been with them all that long, but they have been the absolute greatest from "Chapter One—Contracting the Author's Baby" to "The End." Thank you so much for taking a chance on me!

CHAPTER ONE

(*For immediate distribution*)
TRAVEL ADVISORY: NORTHERN IDAHO
INTERSTATE 90, STATE HIGHWAY 95
Wednesday, May 9, 2057

The Idaho Transportation Department, in conjunction with the Washington State Department of Transit and local authorities, has issued a travel advisory for northern Idaho and parts of northeast Washington. There have been reports of extreme violence between the local Aryan Brotherhood and a marauding nomadic motorcycle gang that has drifted into the area. The aggression has included multiple drive-by shootings of established compounds as well as nomadic encampments on both public and private land.

INTERSTATE 90, STATE HIGHWAY 95
EXTREME CAUTION IS ADVISED
WHILE TRAVELING IN THIS AREA!

Any sighting of the Lichii Ba'Cho Nomads should be reported to the police immediately! They are predominantly of American Indian descent and are identified by small feather tattoos at the corners of their eyes. Their patch is red on black, a stylized wolf's head with "Lichii Ba'Cho" across the top, and a rocker patch beneath with "Established 2025."

INTERSTATE 90, STATE HIGHWAY 95
DO NOT ENGAGE!
THEY ARE ARMED AND EXTREMELY
DANGEROUS!

* * *

"Thanks for the update, Mindy." She looked at the agenda before her. Scanning the conference table, she noted a smug grin on one man's face. "Hal, how's your project going?"

"It's finished."

Sitting straighter, she ignored the gentle murmur from the others present at the weekly staff meeting. "Completely?"

Hal nodded, his grin widening on his homely face. "Yeah. I just got the last of the tests back an hour ago. The programs and counter programs are ready to go whenever you're ready."

"That is outstanding!" She slapped the conference table with one hand, wishing she could express her exuberance in a more natural way. Dancing on the table was frowned upon in the corporate world. *One has to make do.* "It works as expected?"

"Oh, yeah." Hal gave a rueful chuckle. "I've totally pissed off Acquisitions with this project."

"I'll bet you have." She touched her wrist, bringing up her personal calendar. As she waved her hands in the air before her, she canceled and pushed back various meetings, creating a block of time. "I want to see you in my office immediately after this with a full report."

"You got it, boss."

She dropped the screen, and forced herself to return to the agenda. Her team had worked for three years on this project. The desire to rush through the final stages almost overcame her common sense. Yet now was the time to be even more cautious than before. This project had to succeed if this country were to survive. "Daphne? How's the Corporate Export Regulation Division doing this week?"

* * *

(Excerpt, New York Times Data Sheet, Thursday, May 10, 2057)
Are you prepared for the ride of your life?
Danger!
Disaster!
Excitement!
If you're ready for life on the edge, than look no farther than
SynFl™

SynFl™ (also known as the "Synthetic Feeling Engine"), pronounced "Sinful," is the newest in entertainment hardware! Cutting-edge cybernetics deliver the most vivid experiences directly to your prefrontal cortex! The unit is installed during an outpatient procedure and is ready for use immediately! The data input slot lies unobtrusively behind your right ear, cunningly hidden by a mole-like flap of pseudo-flesh. No one need ever know the secret lives you'll live in the privacy of your own mind!

Here is a list of some of our most popular experiences:

Luna Colony Spacewalk!	Race the Dakar Rally!
The Rio Carnivale!	New Zealand Skydiving!
Surf's Up at Spring Break!	African Safari Hunt!

NEW! Perform at the 2056 Winter Olympics! **NEW!**

Hurry! Call us **NOW** to schedule an appointment!

All restrictions apply. See contract for more information.
Not responsible for medical side effects.

* * *

With a groan, Sam rolled over on her tiny cot and slapped at the irritating alarm screaming into her ear. Her aim wasn't good after four whiskey sours the night before, and it took three tries before the incessant whine stopped. She breathed a sigh of relief and dragged herself into a seated position. Her movement triggered the lights and video unit, both blinking on to brighten her day and keep her informed of the world's activities. Rubbing sleep out of her eyes with one hand, she arched her back and stretched out the other arm, nearly touching the opposing wall of the cubicle she had rented for the night. She swung her feet over the edge of the cot. The video unit was programmed for national news and, as she used her fingers to pull the worst of the tangles out of her short hair, a newscaster discussed the recent troubles in the United States. Some corporation or other had actually had the audacity to declare war on the government, and several experts had been brought in to discuss the matter. "Volume down." The vid-unit obeyed as she braced herself for the coming day. Standing, she turned and shoved the cot into the wall. It disappeared into its slot, leaving her more room to maneuver. A low hum emanated from behind the partition as the mechanism within sucked the used sheets off and sterilized the thin plastifoam mattress. She pulled a smaller drawer out of another wall at waist height and used the tiny sink to splash water onto her face.

Today's the big interview. Drying her hands and face with her personal towel, she rummaged in her rucksack. She changed into a fresh pair of skivvies, tossing the soiled ones into the incinerator chute. Sniffing at the jumpsuit she'd worn the day before, she wrinkled her nose. She donned it anyway, promising herself a stop at a 'suit kiosk on the way to the GovMin complex. As she entertained herself with possible outfits, she pulled a mirror and makeup case from the bag. After several minutes of careful application, she studied her face with approval. Running a brush through her hair, she mourned the lack of credits needed to have included a shower in the price of the room. Being freelance and between jobs was a bitch. Hopefully this interview would pay her enough to not only upgrade her storage capacity, but also buy a few essentials. If it also opened a few doors for future lucrative work, she wouldn't complain.

Sam packed her belongings and glanced around the now bare cubicle. The video still flickered and mumbled, suggesting she buy a popular product that would stave off baldness. "Time to get a move on." She shouldered her rucksack and exited the cubicle.

CHAPTER TWO

Dusky leapt across the creek embankment, its sudden appearance hardly breaking her stride. Behind her, she heard Remy panting. *He's getting too old for this shit.* Ahead, she caught sight of Shake crouching along the water's edge where the creek doubled back across their path. He touched a rock, lifted his head and peered at a mark farther on. Dusky slowed her pace, one ear open for pursuit though they were too far into the Coeur d'Alene National Forest for that to be a serious threat. She reached the next track before Shake did, pausing to examine it. A left boot print, still wet, the sole torn where the little toe would be. Remy's arrival was heralded by a light footfall. Dusky looked up. Using sign language, she gave them direction, and they were off again—past the creek, through a copse of sallow trees. Snarling in silent victory, she spotted their prey ahead of them staggering through a small hollow. With another quick series of hand signals, she ordered Shake to flank left and her uncle right.

They'd been chasing this bastard for two days. Oblivious to the presence of his enemies, he looked the worse for wear as he stumbled through the undergrowth, his clothes soiled and tattered by his wild flight. As Dusky drew near, she smelled urine and the sour sweat of fear. *Good. He has reason to be afraid.* He didn't know how close he was to the end of his life, didn't hear her quiet approach as he huffed along, his feet making more noise than a herd of cattle. Not that many herds of cattle roamed the countryside these days; most protein production in the United States was either vat-grown or crammed into huge slaughter yards of the Midwest. Bushes reached out, snagging the man's clothes as he passed. He'd tied his greasy hair back with a strip of cloth. The long strands had fallen into his eyes anyway, hampering his vision. His camouflage shirt hung open, ripped and stained, the hated patch on one shoulder half torn away to flap with every lurching step.

Dusky vowed to wipe her ass with that patch and mail it to his fucking mother.

He tripped on a tree root, hitting the ground with an audible grunt. Before he could push to his feet, she pounced, putting all her weight between his shoulder blades. The soldier exhaled sharply, filthy hands scrabbling at the dirt in useless terror. Dusky leaned all her weight upon him, pinning him like a bug on display.

"Stay put." Remy spoke loud enough for the struggling man to hear. Her uncle materialized in front of them, the well-worn rifle loosely aimed in her direction.

The soldier froze, easing Dusky's struggle. *Handcuff him?* She decided against the measure. *Much more satisfying to watch him wiggle when I pluck off his legs.* Shake emerged from the forest, his young face hidden behind orange and red stripes. He squatted a few meters away to watch the proceedings, trusting her to avenge them. Remy's warpaint consisted of blue and yellow spots, and he'd braided feathers and fetishes into his beard. Green eyes never left their prisoner, yet he gave her a slow nod. *Time to finish this.*

As much as Dusky wanted to drag this out, make their prisoner suffer for all the misery he and his friends had inflicted on her family, she knew there had to be a quick end. Though her dead called for vengeance—for hot blood to spill over her hands as she skinned her enemy alive—she had an appointment to keep and was being pursued by the law. Regretful, she pulled her Heckler & Koch USP auto-pistol from its holster, the slither of metal against leather louder than the soldier's heavy breathing. Wrapping her free hand in the man's hair, she grimaced at its oily texture. Her knee ground into his back as she turned in place, aimed and shot out the back of his left knee. His scream was welcome, but she nearly lost her balance as he jerked with pain. He wouldn't lie still, so she tightened her grip in his hair and tugged his head back to keep him from throwing her. Grinding the hot barrel of her pistol into his cheek, she leaned forward. "That's for Remy's brother, Ice. My father. The man you crucified for not submitting to your racial dominance."

Her uncle nodded in grim satisfaction, the beads and bone in his beard and hair rattling.

Dusky pulled the pistol away before she could prematurely blow off the soldier's face. This was the last of them; she had to make it count. She turned and shot his other knee, this time better prepared for his violent reaction. "That's for Shake's mother, Lucinda, an old woman your convoy ran down in Post Falls last week."

Across from her, Shake gave the soldier a vicious smile, his teeth startling white against the colors striping his skin.

She pushed off of him, knowing her quarry couldn't escape now. He rolled over, writhing in the bloody dirt, crying in pain. Bits of bone showed through the mangled flesh and filthy pants, and he grasped at his thighs as if wanting to hold the wounds. "You fucking squaw bitch!" he sobbed. "Fucking bitch! All you spics ought to be dead!"

Dusky stood over him, aiming for his head. He clung to the last vestige of his hatred as he glared at her, daring her to finish him off. *Too easy.* She wasn't willing to allow his release so quickly. Better he die in agony, his blood soaking into the sacred earth to replenish what he and his kind had taken from her. She lowered her pistol and shot his manhood. His scream was high-pitched as he rolled onto his side, grasping for something no longer there. Out of the corner of her eye, she saw both Shake and Remy cringe from her judgment. She knew neither would interfere and that Remy, at least, understood why this punishment was bestowed. Shake had been scouting when they'd discovered the final resting place of the last of their people, fortunate to not have seen what this bastard's friends had done to their families.

She pushed the soldier onto his back, foot on his shoulder to keep him in place. Blood loss, pain and exhaustion served to tame him as he whimpered beneath her. "That was for my sister, Camilla." She leaned forward to stare into his face. "She was nine years old. Your people raped her to death three days ago." Finally she saw shame as he closed his eyes and turned his head. Satisfied, she holstered her pistol and pulled her knife. With three quick movements, she scalped him, holding it up for the others to see. It was easier to do than she'd thought, glad that Remy had given her pointers before this encounter. "This is for the Lichii Ba'Cho, the Red Wolves. Your Aryan Nation is dead, just like you are. We prevail; you're shit."

Dusky tied the filthy hair to her belt. She remained long enough to rip the offending patch from his shoulder and spit in his face before walking away. Moments later, she trotted into the wilderness, leaving him to the tender mercies of her people. When they finished with him, they'd follow. They were her clan, her blood, and she their chief. She'd wait at the motorcycles for their return.

Justice had been served.

CHAPTER THREE

Sam got off the public transport tram in the center of Vancouver, British Columbia. She gave her datacomm a quick glance, accessing the GPS signal, and proceeded west toward the Canadian GovMin complex. Pedestrians, bicycles and electric cars crammed the streets. Blinking neon vied for consumer attention, their lights as garish as if it were full dark. A colorful mix of people filled the sidewalks—stodgy business folk in their designer suits of the day, people in utilitarian jumpsuits much like Sam's and a colorful rush of teenagers with neon hair and the latest cyber-rage of cat's eyes and whiskers. On the outskirts, near the alleys stood the occasional booster gang member, slinking around in leather and enhanced musculature, sporting blatant metallic limbs and cyberwear. It was too early in the day for the real freaks to be up and around yet.

She passed a full-sized interactive panel, drawing to a halt as it depicted a pristine 2023 Suzuki Hiro-Masuka Special in midnight blue. The picture faded into darkness, and "MOV" flashed three times before the words "Museum of Vancouver, Archaic Automotive Exhibit" slowly reappeared. In small print below, it gave dates for the exhibit, hours of operation and price of entry. Sam sighed. Canada had adopted an electric-only vehicle system twenty years ago, first by banning the sale of petroleum-based automotives. Laws had become more stringent as time had passed, and now it was illegal to build or maintain most combustion engines. *I need to find another hobby before I get arrested.* Shaking off the thought, she continued on her way.

The GovMin complex was a series of staunch gray buildings covering four city blocks. Here the hue of pedestrians shifted, the vibrant colors of the younger crowd all but disappearing in favor of impeccable business outfits. The difference was striking enough for her to worry whether she'd made the wrong choice when she'd chosen the dark blue jumpsuit from the kiosk on her way here. The color was just light enough to make her stand out in the crowd of people waiting for admittance into the Admin building.

In the foyer, she was split off from the workers, queueing behind a much smaller crowd of visitors. At her turn, she put her rucksack on the conveyer for examination and awaited instruction to pass through the scanner. *Do I want a job here?* The idea of having to go through this rigamarole on a regular basis put a damper on the idea of having a steady job. She put her hands up and turned sideways so the scanner could get a good image, glancing once at the workers slipping past security with their ID cards and minimal checks. *I guess if you pass the background check it's different.*

"Okay." The guard, a burly fellow dressed more for a riot than an office job, waved her forward with a meaty hand. "Destination?"

"Communications Department. I have an appointment with…uh…" Sam paused a second, fleeting panic in her mind as she tried to recall the information. Her phone was in her rucksack, and she had the Terminator glaring at her with suspicion. "Robert. Robert Barry."

"Name?" The behemoth looked at a datacomm, a thick finger scrolling through the day's appointments.

Another split second of panic. "Sam Elias." She blew out a breath, feeling silly for almost forgetting her own name.

He held his hand out. "ID." Fumbling, she produced her ident card and watched him study it with fierce concentration. It must have passed his test, for he handed it back to her and directed her to a small alcove. "Over here, Ms. Elias. Stand against the wall." A line of numbers ran up the side, indicators of height. He moved a camera on its stand, raising it level to her face. "Look into the camera." *Flash.* By the time she could see clearly again, she was on her way to the elevator with her rucksack. She lifted the visitor ident card clipped to her pocket, seeing her upside-down visage—short blond hair, wide blue eyes and a slight expression of befuddlement on her face. *One seventy-five centimeters? I need lower heels.*

It took her forty-five minutes, four more security checks and three waiting rooms before she was ultimately escorted into an office that wasn't much bigger than the cubicle where she'd spent last night. A small desk with two chairs adorned the room, with a state-of-the-art computer contrasting the drab appearance. The only attempt at ornamentation was a potted plant. Left alone, she sat in the available chair to wait. Surreptitiously, she reached out and touched the plant, admiring the texture of it. *Wow! It's real!* She resisted the urge to filch a leaf, forcing her hand into her lap. Despite the tiny size of the office, owning a real potted plant in this age of nearly total environmental breakdown was a sign of wealth and power. It scared her a little. She wondered what this job would entail if someone this high up the governmental hierarchy was involved.

She didn't have long to speculate. The door behind her opened, and a man entered. He wore his brown hair short and neatly groomed, with a slight touch of iridescent hair gel to indicate he was still young and in touch with the younger set. His jaw was chiseled, and he wore his sideburns to a point along his cheekbones. "Sorry to have kept you waiting, Ms. Elias." He smiled and offered his hand. "Thank you for coming. I'm Robert Barry."

The touch of cool metal met her touch. She looked down to note the cybernetic limb. "Please, call me Sam."

"Of course. Sam." He gestured for her to remain seated as he sat at his desk. "If you'll excuse me for just a moment." His smile was apologetic. "I haven't quite had time to review your file." He logged in to his computer, clicking at the keypad.

"No problem." She utilized the time to study him. He was good looking and had a well-polished air about him. Though he was probably ten years older than she, the sideburns suggested he hadn't become a stuffy old politician just yet. He exuded an intense calm and pleasantness. She wondered if he was on the political track. The lack of data implants would stand him in good stead with the traditionals, yet the cyberarm would give him an edge with the wetware crowd. He had that winning smile and "real people" look going for him.

He looked up from his files, interrupting her perusal. "You've come about the courier job. Do you have any idea what it's about?"

"Actually, no." She gave him a rueful grin. "A friend of mine has taken work through GovMin—Trace Foster?" He nodded in acknowledgment of the name, and she continued. "He was already on another assignment when this job came up on the GovMin data stream. He's the one who suggested I apply."

"Have you been in this line of work for long?"

She wished she could elaborate the truth a little, but chances were that he had her entire life on that computer screen before him. Lying would guarantee she wouldn't get the job, and she had bills to pay and a need to eat. Besides, getting a government contract—even on a short run like this—could net her more work in the future. "About a year."

"I see." He flicked through more computer files. "And how many jobs have you completed?"

"All told, I've had six runs. The first three were minor. The latest one, however, was a two-fifty gig file for Consumer Affairs." She reached into her rucksack for a data sheet. "If you'd like a copy of my résumé—"

"No, that's quite all right. I have it here." Robert indicated his computer screen. "How much storage capacity do you have?"

"I hold up to five hundred gigs at present. More if it's compressed." She refused to fidget under his frank perusal, drawing upon years of fighting for what she needed to succeed as she smiled back with confidence. He didn't need to know she trembled so hard inside that she felt she'd explode at the slightest provocation.

Robert straightened in his chair. "I think we can take a chance on you. Your records are in order and the references you gave us all attest to your dependability and professionalism." Before she could react beyond her eyes widening, he raised his hand. "You haven't heard the details, yet. You still have time to turn the job down."

Fat chance! "I doubt I will, but give me the details."

"We need you to transfer approximately a terabyte of compressed, highly classified data. It'll be encrypted. Transportation and security has been set up. You'll be entering the United States for delivery to Boise, Idaho."

Sam blinked. *The States?* The thought of getting her hands on a real combustion engine flashed across her mind. The United States had yet to sign the Saareban Protocol and was one of the largest exporters of automotive materials. "Who'll be my contact?"

Robert smiled at her. "Not until you sign the contract."

Sam madly worked out the details. *The States.* Travel between the two nations was frowned upon; Canada GovMin thought their southern neighbor was a safety hazard to their people and with good cause. The strife between global corporations and Uncle Sam had gone on for decades as the two entities struggled for power. It was a normal news day to see the worldwide results of their guerilla actions against one another wherever they had outposts. "You said transportation and security have been set up?"

"Yes."

"What about the return trip?"

"Transportation is provided. Obviously, security won't be needed at that point."

She made her smile as winsome as possible. "Any chance for a...um...layover?" Robert grinned, and she was glad he understood. An old man would never have made the connection so immediately or looked upon her favorably for her desire to do more than make a data delivery.

Robert cocked his head. "How long a layover?"

"A couple of hours maybe? In Seattle." She rolled her eyes. "I would love to see the open-air market there. I've heard so much about it."

He leaned back in his chair and regarded her. "I'll tell you what. You sign the contract, we send you out tomorrow. I'll reschedule your debriefing back here for six days later. That should give you plenty of time to get back."

"You've got yourself a courier, Robert."

CHAPTER FOUR

Dusky splashed water over her face as she rinsed soap and war paint from her skin. The metal mixing bowl doubled as a washbasin when necessary. Black and white and brown, the dirty water swirled together. It would have been nice to head in to Coeur d'Alene and grab a motel room. A hot shower would hit the spot right now. The war between the Lichii Ba'Cho and the Aryan Nation Brotherhood had made things too hot for that. If she and her companions showed their faces in town, they'd be busted by local law enforcement for every charge they could drum up. What the locals couldn't think of, the Feds would happily offer. It was far too much aggravation to suffer for the simple comforts.

Shake and Remy had already cleaned the war paint off their faces. Remy had gone out to the road to check for pursuit. That seemed unlikely. By all accounts, the Aryan army had been obliterated, but who knew how many sympathizers they had in the area. Better to have someone check than suffer a surprise attack. Travel advisories hadn't mentioned that the Brotherhood had instigated the violence, that they had been just as dangerous as their Indian counterparts. No. There had been no mention of the bar fight turned fatal three weeks ago when four of their members murdered Chavez and his girlfriend. Only the Ba'Cho had been mentioned in the news, meaning there were plenty of racist assholes in this area to make trouble for them despite the successful destruction of the Brotherhood. She dumped the dirty water.

Shake sat at the campfire, cleaning his weapons. He'd braided his long hair, wrapping the plaits in orange woolen cloth. A clean towel lay out before him, the pieces of his pistol laid out upon it with military precision. He scrubbed at the barrel with an oiled rag, smiling as Dusky approached. "What are you going to do with that?"

Dusky looked at the scalp hanging from her bike. "Damned if I know. I'll have to ask Remy if he knows what to do. The skin's going to start rotting soon." She put the mirror and bowl away in her bags.

"Don't need to keep the skin."

She looked up to see Remy nearing. "What do you mean? Just cut the hair off it?"

He holstered the rifle in a sheath attached to his motorcycle. "Pretty much. You'll want to tie the hair as close to the skin as possible. Wash it in hot water, cut it off near the skin. Keep the hair for whatever."

Dusky frowned. "Is that what they did in the old days?"

Remy grinned. "Hell, I don't know. That was way before my time, youngster."

Both she and Shake smiled. "If you say so, old man."

He snorted and took a drink from his canteen. "So, where to?"

"Far from here." Dusky made a gesture to Shake, and he quickly reassembled his pistol. "I want to put some miles between us and this place before nightfall. We'll make plans then."

"Sounds good." Remy climbed astride his bike, capping the canteen and putting it away.

Shake put away his gear, dusting off the seat of his pants when he stood up. "Colors?"

Dusky gave the question some thought. With the advisory out against them, anyone seeing their jackets would call the law. She'd be damned if she'd run from the field of victorious battle with her tail between her legs. "Colors. We're Lichii Ba'Cho, the Red Wolves. We're wild and fierce. Fuck anybody who has a problem with it."

"Yeah!" Shake stuffed away his gear and grabbed his earbuds.

She donned her own earbuds and mic and started her bike. The wireless unit connected with her companions. "Let's go. Remy on point." She heard the rumble of her uncle's voice acknowledging her order, and Remy led them out to the road. Music threaded into her ears as Shake turned on his road playlist. The music was welcome, a reminder of good times as they traveled across country with their family. It didn't matter that they were all the family they had left.

* * *

Remy watched his niece through the flames of their fire. Her hair was loose about her shoulders, and she had changed from the leather pants and jacket to a pair of soft trousers and an oversized sleeveless shirt. Four tiny feather tattoos adorned the skin outside the corner of her right eye, denoting her rank within the clan. Her expression was distracted as she diligently cleaned her pistol. *So much like her father. So much hardship.* It was hard to reconcile this stoic young woman with the joyous child he had helped raise. He entertained himself for a moment with his memories.

"What's so funny, Uncle?" Dusky's smile held a hint of puzzlement.

"Nothing. Just remembering a young girl I used to tickle attack every once in a while." Remy reached out a hand to Shake, taking the whiskey bottle from him. He had a swig and passed it to Dusky.

Her smile changed to a rueful grin as she accepted the bottle. "Wouldn't give you any great odds on getting away with it now." She took a swallow of the amber liquid and returned it to Shake.

Remy laughed. "Nope, neither would I."

"So, what are we gonna do now, Dusky?" Shake was all of sixteen, almost a man and eager to get on with developing into one. Remy wondered what the future would hold for him now. *No family, no clan, no Sun Dance.* That would hurt the most. This was the year Shake was scheduled to dance with the Sun and proclaim his adulthood. The Lichii Ba'Cho had always shown *Wakan Tanka* its due, ever since the people had first banded together with her father before she was born. But there was no one to bless the ceremony, no elder to call on the spirits to see the sacrifice he made for his family. *No family at all.*

Dusky's smile faded. "We need to get over to the Pacific tribes and stop their fighters from coming." She gave them an idle shrug. "Waste of time and effort since the job's done."

Shake nodded, and Remy stared into the flames. They had been sent on a mission to the Confederated Pacific tribes, given a mission to search for help with their battle against the Aryans. They had returned to find their people destroyed. It had been Dusky's first official mission for her father—a diplomatic request that she'd successfully brokered without her uncle's help. Fifty fighters had been arranged to arrive within the week. "After that, who knows? Maybe head south, see if we can pick up with another tribe—"

"No." The youths looked at him, their now solitary tribal elder. "We're Lichii Ba'Cho and we stay Lichii Ba'Cho. My brother, Ice, built this tribe from the ground up. Our people escaped corporate servitude and the reservations. We're wolves, not sheep. We recruit." He glanced at Shake. "We find you a strong wife." He smirked at the teenager's blush. Turning his gaze to his niece, he continued, "And you a good husband."

Dusky grimaced and returned her attention to her weapon, shaking her head. "Ain't gonna happen, Uncle. So don't hold your breath."

They had had this argument many times over the last two years, and it was even more important now that young Camilla was gone. "You've got to produce an heir, Dusky." Remy sighed. "Our family is dead."

"I've told you that I will. My way. No husband. No marriage. No one, got me?" Her eyes snapped, the silver cybernetic one flashing in the firelight as she glared at Remy. Slapping her .45 back together, she loaded it, stood and stalked into the darkness.

Remy sighed and stared into the fire. He reached out a hand, the bottle slipping comfortably into it, and had another drink.

CHAPTER FIVE

*(Transcript excerpt, "BiG BiZ BuzZ TalK,"
aired Friday, 5/11/57)*

Alphonse Tresco: Mega corporations have suffered serious credibility issues since the Occupy backlash of the twenty-tens. If you recall, two years after the Occupy movement triggered a worldwide protest, Congress passed multiple regulations to curb corporate excess.

Davson Del Layne: Saving their collective hides, more like.

AT: Be that as it may, mega corporations were almost obliterated in this country as a result.

Martha Montross: And it's taken them the better part of three decades to rebuild.

AT: Yes! Exactly!

DDL: But the question remains—how is Congress dealing with this resurgence of their capitalist opponent?

AT: Poorly.

MM: Agreed. It will take another twenty years of lobbying before corporations will be able to enjoy the freedom they once had in the twentieth century. They haven't been sitting idle all this time, either. They've been working the system, slipping through loopholes whenever they can.

AT: Have you heard the rumor that the mega corporations have declared war against the United States government?

MM: Yes, I did. Do either of you know if there is any credence to it?

AT: I've only picked up the rumor, nothing solid.

DDL: I can't name my sources, but I'm under the impression that several companies got together earlier this year for a business summit. In India.

MM: I think the whole thing is ridiculous. How can a business declare war on a government? That would make your consumers the collateral damage.

AT: Well, it's not like the corporations don't have state-of-the-art firepower and the tactical experience. Didn't Azteca literally take over Yemen in the Middle East four years ago?

* * *

Sam cheerfully made her way to the GovMin complex, a spring in her step as she bypassed a gaggle of preschoolers out for a morning jaunt with their caretakers. With the signing bonus she'd received yesterday, she'd been able to splurge. This morning's private shower felt so much better than a sponge bath. She'd done the smart thing and avoided the bars this time. Not bearing the brunt of excess meant a brighter outlook this morning as she entered the same building as she had the day before. Despite her contractual obligations with Canada GovMin, she was still processed as a visitor. It took another hour of waiting in line, security checks and escorts before she reached her destination: the Communications Department Computer Lab.

"Sam! Good morning." Robert's smile was infectious, promoting her opinion regarding his political aspirations. That kind of smile had to be bought and paid for. Robert indicated the frumpy-looking man wearing a lab coat and standing beside him. "This is Dr. Northern. He'll see to your upload this morning."

She smiled. "It's a pleasure to meet you, Doctor." Though balding and bespectacled—why would anyone want to wear glasses with the current advances in corrective surgery?—Northern's face was unlined. *Must be the geek style.*

"And you, Ms. Elias." He shook her hand and guided her toward a rack of computer terminals.

"I'll meet you afterward with your travel arrangements." Robert gave a slight wave and left.

With the upload now imminent, Sam felt a flutter in her abdomen and chest. She'd never had problems, but the danger of overload was always a possibility. A faulty wire or improper coding in the download application could fry her processor. The fact that this data was compressed to fit her capacity increased the likelihood of an issue. She sat in the chair while Northern prattled on about computers, data storage and cybersystems. Most of his talk was beyond her scientific knowledge; she was a courier, not a computer dweeb.

"What processor do you carry?"

"A Mitsubishi 22X." She gave him a crooked grin. "Not top of the line, but I'm saving my credits for an upgrade."

Northern's hands weaved and danced before him, telling her that he had wireless access to one of the computers here. *Typical geek—livewire Smartlink to computers, probably with all the bells and whistles, but suffering crappy eyesight.* "Your file says you have five hundred gigs of storage, right?" She indicated yes with a nod. "Fortunately, we've refined our compression techniques. There shouldn't be a problem with the amount of data we're uploading. Won't even cause a headache." His fingers dabbled in front of him as he hummed softly. After several minutes, he handed her a cable and slid an old-style keypad toward her. "There you go. Just hit 'enter' when you're plugged in." He moved away. "I'll be available if there are any hiccups."

Sam settled back into the chair. With practiced hands, she brushed her hair away from the port located just beneath the bone under her right ear. The cable easily slipped into it. Taking a steadying breath, she reached for the keypad and braced herself. *I hate this part.* She closed her eyes and hit the button.

While data transfer wasn't a painful process, it remained an uncomfortable task. Try as they might, cyberwear developers had been unable to completely impede the biological and physiological responses that occurred when large amounts of bits and bytes were transferred through brain matter. As with any foreign object inserted into the human brain, the body fought back in a number of ways. In order to use the processor installed inside the brain case, microfilament was used as a transfer medium. There was always energy bleed-off. In the case of couriers running digital data around the world—a much safer prospect than entrusting files to the vagaries of the Internet—that meant heightened senses, faint pressure or throbbing in the temples and the occasional bout of what could only be termed "seasickness." It was something that had to be lived with in this line of work. Sam stoically bore the irritation, hoping that her future upgrade would cause less discomfort. Several of the newer processors coming out purported to have found a way around the human immune system.

Minutes later, upload complete, Sam opened her eyes. She squinted at the brightness of the room. This always happened a few moments after the 'load. Using a meditative technique, she breathed easily until the sensitivity cleared away. As her body returned to normal, she reached up and removed the cable, covering her port with the flap of pseudo-flesh. "All done."

"Good," Dr. Northern beamed as he approached. "Any problems?" He peered at her with intense curiosity.

"Nope, nothing unusual."

He did a cursory examination of her, checking her eyes and throat and testing her blood pressure. "Everything looks good." His hands dashed about the air in front of him as he checked his computer files. "And the upload has been completed from our end. You're good to go." Smiling, he shook her hand. "Robert is waiting for you in the next room. Good luck!"

Robert leaned against the empty reception desk outside. "Good to go?" he asked, standing as Sam joined him.

"Fantastic. Loaded and ready to hit the road." *I'm going to the States!*

"Outstanding." He picked up the thick packet of papers, turning to open it and lay the documents out on the desk. "Here are your travel vouchers for entry to and exit from the United States. We have a team of Mounties waiting for you outside. They'll escort you to the border and hand you off to the US Army."

Army? As much as she wanted to ask, Sam kept her mouth shut. A courier didn't ask questions, didn't poke and pry. That was the difference between a professional and a zero. One did the job and built a good reputation; the other lost credibility and opportunities.

"You'll notice that your re-entry date is two weeks out." Robert gave her a sidelong look. "So long as you return before then, you're covered."

"Frigid!" Visions of experiencing the American lifestyle up close and personal danced through her mind's eye.

He chuckled, sliding another document toward her. "This is your vehicle rental permit. We've contracted with Avis for a car. It'll be a gas guzzler..." He paused, and Sam jumped to reassure him.

"Oh, that's okay. I know the US isn't compliant with the Saareban Protocol."

Robert shrugged. "All right. I just don't want you getting to Boise and not wanting to drive a combustion engine back."

"I'll be fine."

He nodded, returning to the paperwork. "The army will take you to Seattle. From there you'll cross Washington on Interstate 90 into Idaho. I believe they'll be taking back roads and state highways down to Boise from there. Your contact there is Lt. Colonel Gina Conway. She'll set you up for the download."

Just to be certain, Sam repeated what he'd told her. "What about payment?"

He handed her a credstic, a strip of polymer that encased a tiny wireless data processing unit. "Here's half your fee, plus a couple hundred for expenses. The rental car is already paid for, but you'll need this stic to pick it up. Once I have confirmation from Conway that the download was successful, I'll transfer the balance into this account."

Sam smiled as she took the credstic. "Excellent."

"Well, let's get you going."

Grinning ear to ear, Sam followed Robert, daydreaming about her upcoming adventure.

CHAPTER SIX

"Fall in!"

The platoon hastened to obey, though not with the urgency found in a basic training unit. These were all seasoned soldiers with at least one military action under their belts. Sergeant Cunningham stood before the formation, hands on her hips as she surveyed her charges. From the corner of her eye she saw the lieutenant and staff sergeant approach. Dropping her arms, she bellowed, "Attention!" Even her usual laggards hopped to, and she felt satisfaction that they'd put on a good showing for their senior officer and non-com.

"Are they ready, Sergeant?"

"Always ready, Staff Sergeant."

"Outstanding." The lieutenant turned to address the platoon. "At ease." The soldiers relaxed their rigid stances. "I hope everyone enjoyed the late start this morning. We're doing a little mobile guard duty today, and you know how it is with civilians." There was a general rumble of amusement or disgust. "We're picking up our cargo at the Canadian border and transporting it to Boise, Idaho. We have five Humvees and three trikes to get us there. It should be a walk in the park. I'll leave the specific assignments to Sergeant Cunningham. Any questions?"

"What's the cargo?"

The lieutenant grinned. "A Canadian courier. And no, I have no idea what the courier is carrying."

Five Humvees and a platoon for just a courier? Cunningham couldn't help but wonder about the amount of firepower requested for this run. "What about enemy activity, Lieutenant? Anything on the wire?"

"As of right now, Intel hasn't found anything solid. This might have slipped beneath the corporate radar. I'm told it'll be an easy run." A few of the younger and more daring soldiers grimaced at his comment, but wisely didn't voice their dissatisfaction at a babysitting caper. Those with more age and experience took the news with stoicism. Too many times they'd been told an objective would be simple only to lose sweat, blood and comrades in the taking of it. The lieutenant turned to Cunningham. "I'll be in the lead vehicle; assign the squads how you want them. I'll met you at the motor pool." He turned away, the staff sergeant following him.

Cunningham came to attention and saluted. Turning to the platoon, she ordered them to attention. "Let's go then. Right…face. Forward…march!"

* * *

With Robert's assistance and her government-issued travel vouchers, Sam got through the Canadian-United States border with a minimum of fuss. Other people were held back for a variety of reasons, some excuses seemingly pulled out of thin air. She was introduced to an army lieutenant, promptly forgetting his name as he escorted her out of customs.

My first step on American soil. She barely heard the officer who presented her to a sergeant and left. Cunningham had an irascible and abrasive attitude, her lips curved into a permanent sneer. "It's a pleasure to meet you." She held out her hand and was rebuffed.

Cunningham snorted and turned away. "Follow me, Ms. Elias."

Sam frowned at the woman's retreating back, then shouldered her rucksack and followed. She was escorted to a Humvee. Unable to help herself, she let her fingers caress the metal. *What I wouldn't do to get a look under the hood.* Up until it had become illegal in Canada, she'd built her own engines in her spare time. It had been too long since she'd seen a well-constructed combustion engine in action. A quick glance at the impatient Cunningham ruled out asking for the opportunity. *Maybe when we stop for a break.*

Sam climbed into the backseat, noting the torn canvas covers and archaic equipment on the front dash. *This thing's older than I am.* Two men rode in front. The driver was so young, Sam was sure he'd lied about his age at enlistment. The other rode shotgun in the most literal sense of the word. He held a rifle, the barrel sticking up out of the open window. With his free hand, he ran a knuckle across his thick black mustache. Something about him struck Sam as arrogant. Maybe it was the matching sneer he shared with the sergeant or the way he dismissed the driver's opinions with such ease. Sam took an instant dislike to him. The radio crackled with traffic back and forth between the vehicles, and a pair of motorcycles roared off as advance scouts. The man with the rifle, PFC Line, talked sports with the driver, Private Notus. Discussion veered off into a recent military exercise. Sam tried to keep up, but their conversation was incomprehensible to her. Instead she stared out the window until the go-ahead was given. She sat up to get a better look out her window as they convoy rolled away from her homeland.

"First time?"

Sam glanced at Cunningham, not liking the ever-present smirk. "Yes. I've never been to the States before."

"Ah, a virgin."

Line snickered at the sergeant's tone, and Sam frowned. "That just makes me all the more valuable, doesn't it?"

The smirk deepened, slowly becoming a begrudging smile. "Indeed it does."

Pleased she'd scored a point, Sam looked back out the window. The scenery here wasn't any different than what she'd seen on the other side of the border. It seemed somewhat anti-climactic, and she chastised herself for feeling so. The United States was a big country, just like Canada. It would take a few hours for the environment to change.

"Any idea what you're carrying?" Notus asked.

Before Sam could respond, Cunningham intoned, "Ours is not to question why, Private."

Both Notus and Line responded in unison. "Ours is but to do or die."

Sam's gaze flickered between the three of them, puzzled. *Bizarre.* No one said anything more. Cunningham pulled out a datacomm and began working on something. Notus remained focused on the road, and Line scanned the tree line. Ahead of their vehicle Sam saw two Humvees and knew that two more followed. A trike roared past in the opposite direction, running to the tail of the convoy. For the first time she wondered what it was that she carried that required this amount of security.

It was midmorning. With no conversation forthcoming and hours to go before a break, Sam settled down. She fiddled with the earring in her left lobe. The "jewel" was a computer chip holding prerecorded music that had been spliced into her aural nerves. The strains of the latest popular Canadian music filled her ears at such a deep level, no one else detected the sound. She stared out the window, watching the scraggly forest pass.

CHAPTER SEVEN

At midafternoon, the sun had passed its zenith. The trio of Ba'Cho watched from their hiding place among the rocks along a ridge. Remy used a pair of binocs, watching a column of eight vehicles approach the foothills.

"Looks like Uncle Sam." Shake spat to one side.

Dusky nodded, the cyberoptics in her one eye powerful enough to pick up the markings on the sides of the vehicles. "Fort Lewis from the looks of it. Wonder where the hell they're going. They're a long way from home."

"Back roads too." Shake held out his hand, and Remy passed the binocs to him. "They usually run the highways."

Scanning the surrounding countryside, Dusky debated their next move. Having enjoyed a leisurely morning at a closed campground, the Ba'Cho had only been on the road for an hour or so. They'd picked up what appeared to be troop movement only fifteen minutes ago, the trail heading west. "They're heading east, so they're not the ones who left the tracks."

Shake pointed to the left. "They did." Another column appeared out of the tree line, rumbling across the field on an intercept course for Uncle Sam's convoy. There were three vehicles, each emblazoned on the side with a blue eye in the center of a red triangle.

"Corps!" Dusky swore. While there was no love lost between the Lichii Ba'Cho and Uncle Sam, corporations were anathema. The bastards "recruited" downtrodden masses for cheap labor, effectively re-creating indentured servitude. Those that put up a fight for better treatment disappeared— no muss, no fuss and no loose strings. Her eyes narrowed and she chewed the inside of her mouth as she thought furiously. "Come on. Let's get closer." She cautiously crawled backward from the ridge, her pack mates following. Seconds later, the three Ba'Cho roared down the dusty road, weapons within easy reach.

It was time for war.

* * *

Sam drowsed in the heat of the Humvee. Little had been said between the others for hours, and this vehicle didn't have air conditioning. The rest break they'd taken an hour ago had been all too brief, and Cunningham had nixed Sam's request to look at the engine. Sam spent her time listening to music, daydreaming about Seattle and wondering what Boise would be like. Her musings were interrupted by a short burst of static coming from the radio.

"...Repeat...Corps approach from three o'clock! Heads up!" The staccato of gunfire rattled over the radio, echoed in real time from the right. Notus paled, his freckles standing out. The Humvee in front sped up, and he hit the gas to keep pace. Line brought his rifle to his shoulder, sighting three white vehicles driving toward the column. Sam, heart in her chest, wondered why he didn't fire. Cunningham grabbed

Sam's shoulder and shoved her down, drawing her pistol as she forced Sam to the floorboard. Another burst from the radio, this one sounding like the lieutenant's voice. "Bug out! Bug out!" In response, Sam's driver poured on the gas and veered away from the fight as two of the Humvees turned toward the oncoming vehicles.

With Cunningham's attention on the arriving vehicles, Sam rose to her knees and peered over the edge of the back window, watching the superior corporation firepower chew up the military escort. A Humvee exploded, tossing shrapnel into the air with a roar and flash of orange fire. *That was the lieutenant.* Unaware that her mouth had dropped open, she stared at the carnage. The radio on the dash crackled with orders from the staff sergeant, directing his platoon. More weapons fire rattled off as another Humvee opened up with machine guns. An anti-tank missile was launched into a corps truck, its explosion as spectacular as the one that had destroyed the lieutenant's Humvee. Cunningham roughly shoved Sam back down with a curse. Discretion being the better part of valor, Sam remained down, not wanting to tangle with the diminutive sergeant. She heard the screams of dying people and another explosion. Then there was a whoosh of noise, and their vehicle leapt into the air. With a sickening roll it flipped, tossing Sam about the interior. Line flew out his open window, screaming. Sam felt a sudden pain in her head and blacked out.

* * *

The battle was immediately met and immediately brutal. By the time the Ba'Cho arrived, only three vehicles remained in the fight—two military and one corporation. As Dusky roared down the hillside, she watched the corps riot car take out the soldier that had fired a rocket launcher. He jumped and jerked as rounds ripped his body open before he slumped forward, the launcher pushing down to the roof of his vehicle. The weapon discharged, the explosion ripping through the combat vehicle and blowing its occupants to bits.

The remaining Humvee showed severe damage as it steered erratically along the road, indicating the driver had been hit. With a war whoop and a wide grin, Dusky and her pack mates descended on the remaining corporation vehicle. The three motorcycles circled it, Remy using an old M22A4 machine gun and Shake his HK MP-5 auto pistol. Neither would do much damage against the heavily fortified car. As they distracted the occupants, Dusky came around the back, closing in for a quick pass. She used her teeth to pull the pin out of a fragmentation grenade and lobbed it with perfect aim into a gun port. She whooped again and the three pulled out. The corps vehicle exploded from the inside ten seconds later, coming to a slow, smoking stop.

Shake yelled. "Man! Did you see that? Popped it like a fuckin' zit, man! Totally flatlined!" He pulled up near Remy, who watched the last Humvee slow and plowed into the flaming wreckage of one of its own.

Dusky slowed to a halt, blocking the view if not the sound of another explosion. "Check for survivors. Let's see what we can salvage. Make it fast; you know Azteca will send backup and evac ASAP." She grinned at Shake's enthusiasm. "The sooner we're out of here, the better." She rode off, heading for the wrecked Humvee that was farthest away.

* * *

Sam felt something warm and sticky at her side. She groggily looked down to see a severed hand soaking her jumpsuit. With a shriek, she batted it away, coming to full panicked consciousness. Overhead the seat cushion half-dangled, the sight confusing her. It took several precious moments for her to realize that she lay on the ceiling of the Humvee. The interior aroma was reminiscent of raw hamburger. She gagged as she realized the odor came from blood splashed around and on her. Breathing through her mouth, she coughed at the amount of dust and smoke in the air. She hadn't been unconscious long if the dust hadn't yet settled. The front seat was partially crushed. *There probably isn't much left of Line.* She shuddered, glad she couldn't see anything beyond the wreckage itself. Notus was missing and, if the severed hand was any indication, Sam didn't want to find Cunningham. She heard another explosion and some yelling, but no more gunfire. Gingerly, she crawled out the broken window beside her, crouching beside the ruined vehicle to take stock.

Everything hurt as she eased toward the bumper, peering around at the battlefield. The corporation had won this round. *But why? Why attack us?* No army uniforms moved on the road. Two long-haired men in brown leathers picked through the refuse of a destroyed SUV. She watched as one pulled a pistol and fired it into one of the bodies. Mouth dry in fear, she scuttled backward and looked wildly about, seeing nothing but rocks and scrub brush. Something black and metallic caught her eye. *A rifle!* She darted over and scooped it up. Remembering all the American action shows and illegal first-shooter video games of her youth, she brought the weapon up to her shoulder and sighted down it, aiming for the man closest to her. She pulled on the trigger just as a tanned hand reached out and grabbed the barrel, twisting it out of her grasp.

Sam stared at the young woman before her—slender, long dark hair pulled back in a braid that hung down her left shoulder and wearing brown leathers from head to toe. There was something odd about her eyes. One was an intriguing sea green, and the other a ball of silver. *Cyberoptics.* She wore some sort of headset too, with a micro-mic paralleling her jaw. The sense of timelessness came to an abrupt end as the stranger broke eye contact, glancing down at the rifle she'd taken from Sam.

"You ever fire an automatic rifle before?" Her voice sounded husky, and she spoke with a slight accent. She looked back at Sam.

Mouth dry, Sam felt a flush crawl across her face. She shook her head no.

The woman grinned crookedly and handed the rifle back. She pointed to one side of the trigger guard. "Take it off safety first." She turned her back on Sam, squatting as she returned to the task she'd been engaged in before disarming her.

Frozen, Sam held the rifle in a white-knuckled grip as she realized the stranger was looting Notus's body for ammunition. Warily she watched the woman finish scavenging and stand. The woman looked for her two companions. One waved and she responded in kind. Sam swallowed as the woman turned back to her, partially raising the rifle as she stumbled back a step.

"We have to get out of here now. Azteca will be here any minute." Those strange eyes studied Sam. "Chippin' in with us?"

The question confused Sam for a moment. *Not a hostage. Azteca coming. For me, for what I'm carrying?* Various scenarios ran through her mind, none of them pleasant. "Yes!" The woman nodded and turned away, striding toward a beat-up motorcycle. *A real Harley?* The men had already driven away, up into the Rockies. The woman started the Harley, revving its motor, and nodded her head to indicate the seat behind her. Sam paused, the strangest sensation sweeping over her, like this single choice was a monumental one that would affect her life forever. Then the sensation was gone. She clumsily slung the rifle across her back and climbed onto the bike, putting her hands on the woman's hips. The powerful acceleration was foreign to her, and she yelped, wrapping her arms around the woman's waist. She felt more than heard her savior's laughter. Sam's last sight before leaving the clearing was the smoking ruin of one of the army trikes.

CHAPTER EIGHT

(Excerpt, PartyLife Simulations chat log, Jillio server, Japan, Friday, 5/11/57)

Humbleness: Zed, I tell u, Zombie da way 2 go! Vegetate da enemy.
Zed668: think so?
On1Shock: Zombie pukes, input. chip out, wake up. Zombies da worst proggie in the 'verse.
Humbleness: U ever USE it?
On1Shock: duh.
Humbleness: U lie.
On1Shock: i don't lie, input.
Humbleness: Where u get it?
On1Shock: like im gonna tell u where i gots illegal proggie in public chat. u really r stoopid, input.
Humbleness: Who's the input? I ain't a girl, Oni.
On1Shock: not?

Humbleness: Lol, NOT. i output - i swing low and loose and fulla juice.
Zed668: he do, i vouch for him.
5/11/57, 03:44:12, On1Shock has left the chat room.
Humbleness: Sum zeros believe everything they hear.
Zed668: true dat. Input.
Humbleness: *laff*

* * *

Kenneth Shimizu, regional security chief of the Azteca Corporation, grabbed up a piece of data running across his desktop, scanned it, filed it and sent out a quick memo in reference to it within minutes. The Asian man sat behind a desk in a medium-sized office, his navy blue jumpsuit splashed with heavy white stripes running diagonally across his chest and arms. A cable ran from the port in his right temple to the computer pad before him. His arms and hands moved hither and yon, head turning back and forth, eyes watching invisible movement. To the uninformed, he looked autistic, employing ritual movements that his troubled mind had devised to compensate for his anxiety. In reality, he was hooked into the web, conducting business. Databits vied for his attention, leaping and cavorting, blinking in a wild array of colors. With just a little concentration, his real time office came into view, the desk phone ringing. With a quick flick of his wrist, he accessed his phone line, opening it. "Shimizu," he barked.

"Yes, sir, this is Harrelson, sir."

"Did you intercept the package?" Shimizu sent out another memo and accessed the Canadian Interference file. He listened as he scanned over the information.

"No, sir. They got lucky, sir."

Shimizu snorted in derision. "Lucky? More like incompetent." His voice was sharp as he visually ran through the list of operatives involved. "I want everybody in the field demoted. Let's transfer in some fresh troops from Silicon Valley and call Yemen for backup."

"*Yes, sir.*" There was a pause. "*Sir, there are no operatives in the field. No survivors on this mission.*"

For a tenth of a second, Shimizu froze before continuing his mental and physical manipulations. "Then I guess you'd better hop on that personnel transfer, eh?"

"*Yes, sir.*" Another pause. "*There seems to have been some outside interference—three sets of cycle tracks leaving the area. The courier must have been aided somehow.*"

"Do we have any idea who the courier is?"

"*Yes, sir, I think so. ID/body matchup is pretty consistent. We have personal possessions for Sam Elias, Canadian National, but no body at the site.*"

"Good, good. That's our target. Get those fresh troops in. ASAP!"

"*Yes, sir. I'm on it!*"

The security director severed the connection and brought up a map of the tri-state area. *Time to play hide and seek.*

* * *

"Define 'gone,' Captain."

The officer swallowed, standing a bit straighter. "Gone, General, as in 'no longer responding to radio.'"

General Dan McAndrews rumbled as he pushed back from his desk and came to his feet. "How long?"

"Lt. de Gault's convoy checked in two hours ago outside Coeur d'Alene, Idaho. They had transferred to US 95 and were heading south. They've missed their last two check-ins." The captain swallowed hard. "I requested a flyover from Mountain Home Air Force Base."

"How long ago?" McAndrews brought up the image of a map on his display, a six-by-four-foot touch panel he used for mission briefings. Using his fingers, he zoomed in on the route he'd ordered the courier team to take.

"Half an hour, sir."

"They should be there by now. Get me a visual."

"Yes, sir!"

The captain's eyes glazed over, and McAndrews turned away in disgust. Damn these kids and their cyber-whoozits, sticking computers in their brains and wires into their bodies. *If God wanted Man to mesh with Machine, He'd have given us all dataports at birth.* An upper corner of McAndrews's screen blinked red, and he reached out to touch the pixelated square, brushing it downward. It opened up to a live camera feed, direct from the helicopter flying over the convoy's proposed route.

"They should have already seen them, sir." The captain's hands flickered a moment in front of him, and a blue dot popped up on the map. "That's the location of the air force." A green dot appeared south of the blue one. "And that's where the convoy should be now, but they aren't there."

McAndrews swore, eyes glued to the video feed. "Audio?"

Another moment passed, and the speakers in the ceiling crackled.

"Castle to Rock, I got nothing."

"Neither do I, Cast—Wait. Up ahead. Is that smoke?"

"That's what it looks like, Rock. Let's get a closer look."

McAndrews gritted his teeth. The seconds ticked by as the two officers waited to see and hear what the helicopters discovered.

"Confirm, Castle. I have smoke and multiple damaged vehicles, multiple bodies." The video feed swept in an expansive arc as the carnage was revealed. McAndrews swore again. Rock continued broadcasting. *"Looks like three bikes, five army transports and three destroyed SUVs."*

"Tell them to get a closer look at that burnt-out SUV."

"Yes, sir." The captain went to McAndrews's desk, fluttered his fingers about as he made some arcane connection and picked up the desk phone. His voice echoed over the loudspeaker as he gave the order. "Castle, this is Sea Rain. Close in on the SUV, try to get an ID."

"*Copy Sea Rain, Castle coming about.*" The video swooped as the helicopter banked and came back to bear on the foreign vehicle.

"*Sea Rain, this is Rock. I'm seeing multiple tracks in and out of the area and what looks like a vehicle landing area. Whoever did this had an evac transport on hand. I don't think we'll find any bodies.*"

"Copy, Rock. Castle, what do you see?"

The burnt-out SUV loomed large on the screen as someone zoomed the image. Smoke still billowed out of the wreckage, the damage so severe that McAndrews couldn't even guess at the original color of the thing. "I want them to remain in the area. Get an investigation team together and out there, pronto. No one in or out."

The captain nodded. "Yes, sir."

"And see if we can get some satellite images."

"Yes, sir!"

As he relayed the order to the helicopters and made the arrangements, McAndrews studied the SUV. *Who the hell are you, and how did you know to attack this convoy?*

CHAPTER NINE

Dusky turned off the dirt road, making for an old campground near Winchester, Idaho. It had been slow going as they shadowed the main highway, sticking to country and logging roads, heading south instead of west. The last thing she wanted was to be caught in desert country if Azteca was looking for survivors from their ambush. Better to stick to the mountains and cross into Oregon. They could make for Interstate 84, then head into Portland before turning north. It was a more meandering route, but safer. The Confederated Tribes weren't supposed to send anyone to northern Idaho for a week—she had a few days to catch them before they departed for northern Idaho.

The proximity of her passenger made the detour entertaining. As the bike jostled over ruts and bumps, she felt the woman's breasts press close and the hands about her waist grip her tight. At one point, Dusky realized she'd been subconsciously hitting potholes and rocks on purpose. She felt a wry grin flicker across her face. *Lecherous woman.*

It was time to regroup and get their bearings. She guided her pack mates through the campground, finding an abandoned game trail. Ducking her head, she avoided hanging branches as they plucked at her and followed the trail to a small clearing. Shutting off the bike, she regretfully dismounted, moving away from the *gringa*. Quiet settled over the clearing as Remy and Shake followed suit. "We'll crash here tonight. No open fire after dark. Shake, you've got first watch."

"We're running low on water." Remy pulled his gear off the back of his motorcycle and set it on the ground.

"Let's get a fire started, then. We've got a couple of hours to boil some from the lake." Dusky turned to the woman standing by her bike. Their eyes met, and she saw a flash of white light, like an electrical spark racing along an invisible line between them. The same thing had happened back at the ambush, which was the only reason Dusky had invited this stranger to come with her. She felt an impending sense of… something—excitement, trepidation, dread and relief seemed most prominent, a whirlwind of emotions and dim feelings that scattered her thoughts, leaving her standing with dismay in the eye of the storm. She mentally shook herself, focusing on the here and now. "You ever go camping?"

"Not like this. Only at government-run camps."

Oddly disappointed, Dusky gestured to the center of the clearing. "Clean a spot in the middle here. Get some rocks and build a circle, maybe two feet across." She turned away. "C'mon, Shake, let's go find some wood."

* * *

Sam watched the two bikers disappear into the woods. *His name's Shake. Hers is…Dusky…?* She glanced at the remaining man, the one with a braided beard tinged with gray. He moved efficiently and silently as he unpacked his things, ignoring her. She sighed and built the firepit as ordered.

While she had wanted to experience the rough and tumble United States during this job, she was receiving a much closer look than she'd anticipated. She had no idea why Azteca had attacked the convoy. The majority of the world had made peace with the corporations, but the independent spirit had prevailed in this country, causing a serious rift. The timing of the Azteca assault on US GovMin seemed suspect, but Sam thought the attack could have been an act of convenience— Azteca had come across the army by accident. There was no reason to believe that she'd been the target, despite the encrypted data she carried in her head. That would be just too spy-thriller-vid. Regardless of this setback, she had to get to Boise. Her future employment with Canada GovMin was in danger. If she failed, GovMin could even blackball her across the country, forcing her to work in obscurity for the rest of her life or find another career.

She searched for likely rocks, using her recollection of rustic videos to determine size and placement. *I wonder what it was like here a hundred years ago, before strip mining, slash logging and global warming.* Squatting down behind a motorcycle, she collected a rock, the modern vehicle driving her daydreams to ground. These people were nomads, living day to day, always on the road. She'd heard plenty of horror stories at home. Nomads were bloodthirsty subhumans that indiscriminately killed everyone in their path. They were filthy, overloaded with cybergear, and bristling with weapons. Nomads took over small towns and destroyed them for fun. Parents in Canada used American nomads as threats—"Be good or we'll sell you to the nomads." These three didn't act very bloodthirsty. *Well, except when they're shooting survivors of that fight.* They weren't filthy, just covered with road dust as she was herself. The only evident cybergear was Dusky's eye and the weapons didn't look over the top like some of the more sensationalistic videos had portrayed. Sam tried to imagine these three taking over a small town to rape, pillage and destroy. Despite herself, she snorted aloud.

"Something funny?"

Sam looked sharply at the older man, wondering if she had offended him. His face was closed to her. "Uh…no. I was just, you know, thinking to myself, that's all."

He gave her a solemn nod and finished putting three sleepbags out.

Sam placed the rocks in a circle, leaving no gaps. Finished, she dusted off her hands and stood, awkwardly watching her caretaker. "Maybe I could go get some water?"

"We'll both go." He picked up a medium-sized cook pot and handed it to her, taking a larger one.

They threaded their way through the ragged woods, catching sight of the others loading their arms with deadwood. Emboldened, Sam spoke. "What's your name?"

"Remy."

"You're a nomad, right?" At his distracted nod, she stammered, "What…uh…'group'?"

"We're Lichii Ba'cho."

"I'm Sam." She received an acknowledging nod and nothing more. She wondered if the other two were as reticent conversationalists as Remy. At the edge of a small lake, Remy waded out into the brown water to his knees, past the worst of the muck and debris along the water's edge. With a swipe of his hand, he cleared oily-looking scum from the surface and plunged his pot into the lake. He handed the pot back to Sam and took hers, repeating the procedure. He returned to the shore, stamping his dripping boots before heading back to camp. She trailed behind him, wondering if she'd survive the night. Either the heathens of her fears would murder her, or she'd die of silent boredom.

Shake and Dusky had already returned to the campsite. Dusky had built a smokeless fire while Shake dismantled his auto pistol, laying the pieces onto an old bath towel. As Remy and Sam approached, Dusky rose and took the pot from Sam. "Sit down." She pointed at a sleepbag and turned to set the water to boil, not bothering to see whether or not Sam obeyed. Sam hesitated a moment before complying. When flames licked the side of the pots, Dusky sat beside her and looked at the others. "Well, what'd we score?"

"Got lots of ammo. Picked up another LAW." Shake indicated an olive green tube hanging from his motorcycle. "Only survivor was a corps."

Dusky's silver/green eyes narrowed. "You flatlined him, right?"

Shake nodded with a wry snort. "Of course." He ran small cloth patches through the barrel of his pistol with a metal rod, digging at the powder discharge inside. Sam shivered at the callous reaction from both of them. Shake was barely a teenager, and he acted like killing a human being was just another tedious task.

Dusky nodded her chin at Remy. "You get anything?"

Remy had retrieved his rifle and began to break it down. "Got some good stuff." A slight grin crossed his face, the first expression of positive emotion Sam had seen any of them convey. "We've got food for a few more days. Picked up half a case of MREs from that Humvee that didn't explode." He looked pointedly at a sack by Dusky's sleepbag.

Grinning, Dusky scooped it up and searched inside. "Got me some more ammo. The Humvee wasn't too badly damaged, but all the firepower was in the other ones. Not much else, except her." She pulled a narrow cardboard box out of the bag and handed it to Sam.

Accepting it, Sam didn't know if she should feel insulted or not by Dusky's tone. "Um…thanks." *Go with the flow, Elias. You don't know these people or their ways.*

Dusky pulled a box out for herself and tossed one to each of the men. She ripped it open, a variety of foil-wrapped packets spilling into her lap. Using her teeth she tore open the largest, the automatic heating element igniting upon contact with the air. In seconds, the food steamed. She and her pack mates lost no time in bolting down their meals.

Sam briefly watched, reminded of starving animals. She opened her pouch and sniffed at it, wondering if her judgment of these people had been too hasty. They weren't the savages of news and entertainment outlets, but they certainly weren't angels either. No utensils were provided, so Sam adopted their style of eating, squeezing the food up to the opening. The food ignited her hunger, and she finished the main course in a matter of minutes, table manners be damned. While filling, the main entree wasn't quite enough. She rooted inside the box and found crackers, peanut butter, a packet of strawberry jam and a cookie. As the others finished eating they tossed their packets into the fire, and Sam followed their example. Dusky rose and checked the water to ensure it boiled, adjusting a pot closer to the flame. Sam looked up from her chocolate cookie to find all eyes staring at her. She set the dessert aside and held her chin up, refusing to drop her gaze.

"Who are you? And why was Azteca after you?"

The aftertaste of the cookie soured in her mouth. "My name is Sam Elias. I'm a courier for the Canadian Government Ministry." Her saviors—*captors?*—showed little reaction. "I don't know if Azteca was after me, let alone why."

Remy's voice was soft. "Oh, they were after you, all right."

Dusky reached out, boldly grabbing the back of Sam's head and tilting it one side. She ran a rough thumb over the pseudo-flesh hiding Sam's dataport before letting her go. "You know what you're carrying?"

Sam shook her head no, trying to regain the equilibrium that she had lost with Dusky's touch. It had been like an electric shock. *It's been too long since I've gotten laid, that's all.* She fell back onto her meditative technique to settle herself.

"Where were you heading?"

"To Boise. They've got the codes to unlock the data transfer." Curiosity getting the better of her and irritated with Dusky's attitude of superiority, Sam asked, "Do you work for your government, then?" The three nomads burst into laughter, startling her. Shake laughed so hard, he broke into tears and rolled on his sleepbag, howling. Remy's was a dry chuckle, and Dusky chortled, her eyes dancing merrily. Sam's annoyance raised another notch. "So, you work for another corporation, then?" That elicited even more laughter.

Shake held his sides weakly. "Stop," he begged her. "No more!"

Dusky wiped a tear from her single organic eye, still chuckling. "Oh, that was good!"

Annoyed, Sam felt her skin flush as she glared at them. Dusky met her gaze, her laughter dissipating as she stared back. *She's beautiful when she smiles.* Sam's irritation faded, replaced by a sudden urge to feel those lips against hers, to make them sigh and moan, to hear them call her name. Relief dashed cold water on her unwanted ardor when Dusky turned away to fiddle with the boiling water.

"No, we don't work for either." Dusky set a third pot to one side of the fire. She used worn oven mitts to collect one of the boiling pots, covering it with a thin cloth. With a deft movement, she flipped the boiling pot over the new one, the cloth filtering out the worst of the slime that had boiled to the top of the pot. That finished, she put the new pot back onto the fire.

Sam struggled to dismiss her inappropriate arousal and concentrate on the conversation. *Not mercenaries then.* "Then why were you there? Why did you take me with you?"

Shake put his pistol back together. "We found their tracks and followed. Figured we'd get our licks in when we saw what was going down." He glanced up once at Sam, brown eyes distant from her in ways she couldn't begin to fathom. "You're just lucky enough to be with the military and not Azteca."

Sam remembered him shooting a wounded person and shuddered. *That could have been me!*

Remy's voice broke in to her ruminations. "Stop scaring the poor woman. She's been through enough already."

Shake blushed as he grinned apologetically. Sam responded with a careful nod.

"As for why we took you," Dusky continued, "what the corporation wants, we deny when we can." She poked a stick at the fire, stirring the embers. Her back remained turned to Sam as she shrugged one shoulder. "Besides, I found you. You're mine now."

The silence stretched on for an indeterminate time as the words sank into Sam's mind. "What?" Memories of the old-time vids her mother used to watch welled up within her, where ancient cultures took such obligations seriously. *But this is the twenty-first century! Right?* She stared at Dusky's braid, willing her to turn. When that didn't happen, Sam looked at the men for confirmation. Shake shrugged with a grin, and Remy's face revealed nothing. "What do you mean, I'm yours?" Sam's voice had become high-pitched, and she barely noted the strangled sound it made.

Dusky turned to regard her with a face of stone, one eyebrow raised. "What part of 'mine' don't you understand?" she asked with icy calm.

What the hell? Sam's mind shut down. She sat there, unable to speak. Remy ignored her pleading expression in favor of cleaning his rifle. Shake was no help either. She felt her anger igniting, burning away the stunned ennui. *How dare she? The audacity!* She glared back at Dusky, surprised by a sudden flash as their eyes met. For the second time in less than fifteen minutes, Sam's anger waned, replaced by desire. She looked down at her hands, trying to marshal scattered thoughts and emotions. *What the hell is going on with me?* A featherlight touch at her temple interrupted her thoughts. She looked up. Dusky's face had softened. She appeared apologetic but didn't speak. She brushed Sam's hair back and grasped her right shoulder, wordlessly raising her eyebrows in question. Sam flushed and gave a slight nod. When Dusky released her, she felt bereft.

Dusky turned back to the pots of boiling water. She glanced at Remy. "What?"

Remy shrugged in nonchalance, returning his gaze to his weapon. "Nothing."

Sam's eyes flickered between them, noting for the first time that Remy's eye color matched Dusky's. Rather than ask, she kept her mouth shut, watching as Dusky finished filtering the boiled water and gathered their canteens for refilling. A short time later, three cups of tea steeped on the rocks near the flames. When they were ready, Dusky handed out the cups, her long fingers brushing against Sam's as she passed one to her. Sam's mouth went dry at the tingle rushing up her arm. *Of all the people I get a hard-on for, it's a murderous nomad? What is wrong with me?* She took a shaky breath and blew on her tea to cool it. They sat in silence, drinking tea or deep in thought.

Dusky heaved a sigh and looked at the men. "Shake, I'll relieve you later. We leave in the morning for Boise, get this *gringa* to her destination before heading to the coast."

Shake nodded, sucking his teeth. He stood and moved away from the encampment, into the blighted undergrowth. Remy stood as well, helping his niece put out the fire. Sam remained on the sleepbag, wondering where she would sleep. Her ribald mind conjured all sorts of ideas on that topic, and she hurriedly swallowed the last of her tea, burning her tongue and throat. *Get a grip, Elias.*

Pulling a spare blanket from her saddlebag, Dusky indicated the sleepbag where Sam sat. "You sleep there."

Sam blinked in surprise. She had assumed that she would use the blanket. Apparently, Remy had thought the same as he froze for a second and watched Dusky with narrow eyes. Dusky glared back, and he gracefully turned away, preparing for bed. The glare was turned on Sam, who hastily did the same. *What's that about?*

CHAPTER TEN

(*Spokesman-Review flimsy, Spokane, Washington,
Saturday, 5/12/57, Early Edition*)

Battle Near Interstate 90
42nd MP BDE Slaughtered by Unknown Assailant

An encounter between the United States Army
and an unidentified corporation ended in death in
a clearing off Interstate 90 near Post Falls, Idaho,
Friday afternoon. The US Army Military Police
convoy, led by Lt. Harrison de Gault, had left
Spokane, Washington, only a quarter hour earlier.
Witnesses say the crack military team assigned to
the 42nd Military Police Brigade out of Fort Lewis,
Washington, had seemed in good spirits when they
left the rest break area.

Reports poured in minutes later of heavy explosions and gunfire as a bloody battle erupted in the distance. While there are no eyewitnesses to the massacre, local news outlets received multiple calls from civilians who heard the engagement, many reporting columns of black smoke billowing into the sky. Military officials have begun interviewing individuals regarding the recent hostility between the local Aryan Brotherhood and a nomadic gang that had drifted into the area last month. So far, there seems to be no connection between the notorious Lichii Ba'Cho and the destructive battle.

It is impossible to say how many casualties are involved in this attack. Witnesses say there were at least thirty MPs in the convoy. The US Army has cordoned off the area, detouring traffic as they conduct their investigation. Air Force drones patrol the sky, and no photos of the possible carnage have been made available to the general public.

The battle was one of several clashes that have broken out between the United States military and various corporations in recent months nationwide. The current relationship between the United States and several megacorporations has become more strained over the last three years as Congress has stuck to its guns, supporting current legislation that demands severe restrictions and oversight in corporate financial activity. Several corporations—Plastica, the DiBilio Corporation and Yamaguchi Incorporated to name a few—have been able to lift some lobbying laws, but it's taken them the better part of a decade to do so. Meanwhile, the American people suffer from substandard goods as multiple corporations refuse to do business altogether—

-Story continued, page A2-

* * *

Dusky woke in the predawn, wisps of an erotic dream tickling her memory as well as other parts of her anatomy. She sat up, resting forearms on bent knees, blinking owlishly. Glancing to her left, she saw her sleepbag full of blond *gringa*, the vision hammering the provocative dream home. *Oh, yeah. An overnight stay in Boise is definitely required.* She rose, nodding a greeting to her uncle who had taken the last watch. Folding the blanket, she stowed it before moving away from the campsite. While yesterday's activities weren't out of the norm, the newest addition to their ranks had unsettled her. This strange connection she seemed to have with Sam Elias stirred things up in her soul that she couldn't identify. She needed a workout. She needed to center herself.

Backtracking the game trail, Dusky came out into the campground. She found a concrete slab in a large clearing. It had once been a parking spot for a recreational vehicle, complete with an electric fuse box sticking out of the ground. Though today was a beautiful spring Saturday morning there were no campers in residence. Sheople nowadays rarely took the time to leave their cities and towns for rustic vacations like the old days. Most couldn't afford the equipment and time away from work, and those that had the money preferred ski resorts and foreign beach getaways. That worked out just fine for nomads like the Lichii Ba'Cho, the people who lived nowhere.

Dusky stepped onto the slab, measuring its length and width with her pace. It was of a decent size, though she'd have preferred it to be a bit wider. Untying her hair, she shook out her braid, running her fingers through the strands. She braided it anew, tying it off. After several minutes of stretching, she closed her eyes, seeing the white-hot electric spark from Sam's blue eyes, noting the presence of dimples when Sam smiled. *Concentrate.* She banished the vision and settled into the first kata.

* * *

Sam blearily opened her eyes, staring into the solemn gaze of Remy, who had shaken her awake. "I'm up." She croaked more than spoke and cleared her throat. Remy moved away to kneel by Shake, and Sam pushed herself into a sitting position. She scrubbed her face. *Mornings suck.* The wisps of a very naughty dream tickled her mind, and she looked around for Dusky. Remy had restarted the fire, and Shake was tying his boots. Dusky was nowhere to be seen. *Where is she?* "I'm going to...go. You know."

Shake waved negligently in her direction, and Remy ignored her.

Taking their lack of concern as a positive thing, Sam followed the game trail they'd taken to get there. Several minutes later, she stared curiously around the abandoned campground. *Where'd she go?* She saw movement through the scraggly trees and crept forward. Dusky, eyes closed, danced on a concrete slab. Not wanting to disturb her, Sam moved slowly so as not to make noise. She reached an old picnic table and sat down.

Dusky's muscles rippled as they moved in time to unheard music. Arms and legs weaved in and out with a force that audibly sliced the air. She whirled, her body leaving gravity behind on more than one occasion. At other times, her hand was her only contact with the ground as she spun, head down. The moves were fluid and raw and powerful, not recognizable to Sam as any she'd seen before. As the dance continued, a thin sheen of sweat developed on Dusky's skin, the early morning light making her glow. Eventually the dance slowed, stopped. Dusky panted, eyes still closed.

Mesmerized, it took Sam a moment to return to reality. Realizing she might be intruding, she stood and prepared to go back to the campsite.

"Stay." Dusky's eyes had opened, watching her.

Sam slowly sank down, her skin heating. "I…didn't mean to interrupt."

Dusky shrugged and began her cool-down stretches. "No biggie. I heard you walk up."

Studying her, Sam debated before speaking. "What was that, anyway? I've never seen anything quite like it."

"It's called capoeira." Dusky's breathing had evened out. "It's a form of martial arts that originated with Brazilian slaves in the 1800s." She finished her cool down and padded toward Sam. "The slaves were forbidden to practice their fighting technique so they disguised it as a dance."

"It's beautiful." Sam stood at Dusky's approach. The next words fell out of her mouth before she could stop them. "You're beautiful." She winced internally. *Oh, God! Did I just say that?* Dusky transformed before her eyes from a young woman into a seductive jungle creature on the prowl. With hooded eyes she took a long, leisurely look, and Sam felt the fiery touch of that gaze from the tips of her toes to the ends of her hair. She convulsively swallowed, unable to breathe as the memory of last night's dream ignited her desire. Dusky took a final step, her mismatched eyes settling on Sam's lips, her body a hairbreadth away. Sensing more than seeing Dusky's hand rise, Sam reached out to stop her. *I don't want this.* Again, the fleeting memory of her dream rolled across her mind. *I don't?* Long fingers wrapped around her wrist, halting its momentum. Dusky's other hand took Sam's chin, tilting her head. Despite her inner struggles, Sam's lips parted slightly. As their mouths neared, their breath mingled. Dusky inhaled deeply, sending a rush of arousal through Sam.

"Dusky."

Everything stopped. Sam froze, tensing and rolling her eyes to her right. Remy stood nearby. She returned her gaze to Dusky who had simply stopped moving—a pause rather than a cessation of activity—no stress, no tension evident.

Her expression didn't change and her eyes remained locked on Sam's lips. Sam attempted to break away, to step back, but Dusky held her firm by wrist and chin.

"Yes, Uncle?"

Remy cradled his rifle in his arms. "When do you want leave?"

"After we eat."

Sam saw the mental dismissal, heard the crunch of gravel underfoot as Remy walked away, a jaunty whistle on his lips. Pressure on her chin reminded her where she was, strong fingers giving her a gentle squeeze. Stupefied, she watched as Dusky leaned close. Their lips met, moving together. Dusky's tongue caressed, demanding entry. Sam allowed the kiss to deepen. It was a slow, measured exploration, tongues entwining, familiarizing. Sam melted into it, the tingle burn of arousal blazing a sharp trail down to her belly. Eyes closed, she lost herself in the sensation. She gave herself. Echoing between them were the words Dusky had spoken the night before. *"You're mine now."*

Dusky gradually broke off the kiss, retreating in increments until she nibbled Sam's lower lip, causing Sam to gasp and shiver. Then the connection was gone. Sam opened her eyes, trying to get her bearing. She saw Dusky walking away. She shook her head in an effort to clear it.

"Time to eat."

Sam stood for a few seconds, touching her lips with her fingers. She followed.

CHAPTER ELEVEN

Back at camp, the fire crackled with cheer. Remy squatted beside it, heating the last of the purified water for tea. Shake sat astride his motorcycle, smearing peanut butter onto a cracker. He grinned at Sam and Dusky as they appeared, wiggling his eyebrows in a teasing manner. Sam felt a flush reach her face and silently cursed her light skin color as Shake's lips widened into a toothy smile. Dusky stopped at a satchel by the fire and grabbed two of the MREs scavenged the day before. She tossed one to Sam, barely glancing at her as she settled on the ground beside the fire.

The sudden distant treatment confused Sam. Puzzled, she sat equidistant between Remy and Dusky to eat her breakfast. She hardly tasted the food as she replayed the delicious kiss. It appeared that whatever enjoyment Sam had gleaned from the contact hadn't affected Dusky at all. As she ate her meatloaf casserole, Sam frowned, remembering the way Dusky had shifted into a dangerous, seductive hunter.

I didn't imagine that. The longer she thought about it, the more annoyed she became at Dusky's aloofness. Remy had seen the beginnings of the kiss; Shake obviously assumed something had occurred. Why did Dusky act like nothing had? *Does she think I'm a zero?* Anger smoldered in Sam's heart at the thought that Dusky had so easily dismissed her from consideration. *I'm not a zero, damn it!*

Shake finished his meal, dismounting to toss the wrappings into the fire. "How long we staying in Boise?"

Dusky looked up from the flames. "Long enough to drop her off, I expect."

"Do we have the credits for maintenance?"

Remy held a cup of tea out to Shake. "What's up?"

Shake jerked a thumb over his shoulder. "She's riding a little rough. I might need to have her looked at."

A surge of satisfaction shot through Sam. *I'll show her I'm no zero.* "What do you mean riding rough? You talking sluggish?" They all turned their heads to stare at her as she got to her feet. "Do you have trouble at low or high speeds?"

Opening his mouth, Shake closed it and looked at Dusky. She gave him a slow nod. "High speed."

Businesslike, Sam circled the fire and knelt beside Shake's bike. "I'm guessing you've checked the plugs. You notice any knocking or anything?" She felt a sense of homecoming as she finally got her hands on an engine. "Got any tools?"

Shake, hands on his hips, stared down at her. "I don't think—"

"Give her tools."

Sam looked over her shoulder at Dusky, who now stood by the fire, eyes intently watching. *Hah! Got your attention now, don't I?* Shake opened a saddlebag and retrieved a toolkit, handing it to her. "Thanks." Though it had been a few years since she'd legally worked on a combustion engine, the knowledge and skills quickly returned. While she worked, she chattered away. "What you're describing could be a number of things. It could be firing incorrectly, or the fuel to air mixture is off. Or maybe it's low compression." She checked the plugs, finding them in their proper places with clean and solid contacts. "Any knocking?"

There was a pause before Shake answered. "No. No knocking." He squatted beside her, watching her work. "I thought it was firing wrong too, but I've checked the ignition and pick up coils and the plugs."

She nodded. Working her way past the outer pieces of the engine, she dug deeper into the mechanism. "Any trouble with the brakes dragging or the clutch slipping?"

"No."

"What about the oil? When's the last time it was changed?"

"About a month ago."

"Anything unusual about the viscosity or color?"

"Naw, it was normal."

A serious inspection couldn't be done here and now. Sam chewed her lower lip, peering at the cylinder head. She felt her time in the limelight slipping away. *I need to come up with something, damn it.* "Got a flashlight?" Shake was fully into the moment, absently retrieving a small flashlight for her. She used it to illuminate the cylinder head, running her now dirty fingers over it. The engine wasn't a pristine showpiece; it looked to be as old or older than Shake. Using her finger, she wiped away dirt and grime, revealing pitted metal. "I can't be positive without breaking it down completely, but I think the problem can be either the cylinder head gasket is damaged or one of the valve springs is broken or warped." She twisted around to look at Dusky. "I might be able to fix it if you have the time." Sam grinned at Dusky's expression. *That's right, input. I'm not just a messenger girl.* Dusky studied Sam, that intensity in her eyes again. The look sent shivers down Sam's spine.

Remy and Shake both stared at Dusky too, awaiting her verdict. "Not now. We have to get you to Boise. Azteca doesn't give up so easy; if they're after you, they're going to know you weren't killed in that convoy."

Sam swallowed, fighting her arousal. She turned back to the bike, seating the plugs firmly in place and reattaching wires and cables. "Maybe after I've uploaded my data."

"Maybe. Maybe not. We have someplace else to be."

The words held a finality that Sam didn't like. She finished working and sealed the toolkit, handing it to Shake as she stood. "Okay. The offer's open, though."

Dusky gave a curt nod. "Let's go. Daylight's wasting."

While Shake put away his gear, Remy nodded and kicked dirt over the fire. He handed a cup to Sam as she passed. She thanked him and drained the tea in three swallows. Dusky helped extinguish the fire and packed the last of the gear on her bike.

Fifteen minutes later, Sam held Dusky's waist as the bike crawled down the abandoned game trail, Remy and Shake behind them. She stared at the campground, feeling a sense of loss as they passed the concrete slab where she and Dusky had shared that wonderful kiss. *Elias, you need to get your head in the game.* She reminded herself that she was on a job, that she needed to regain her professional perspective, that when these people dropped her off in Boise she'd never see them again. A lump developed in her throat, and she silently cursed herself. She'd seen too many tragic romance videos. *Mama told me those things would rot my brain.*

Sam forced herself to focus on her goal—Boise, data dump, a car back to Seattle and several days shopping a big American city. There was no room for destructive nomads in her life, especially not the dark beauty in her arms right now.

* * *

The pressure against Dusky's back became stronger as her passenger leaned into her. She glanced over her shoulder. The monotony of the scenery and the steady rumble of the motorcycle had put Sam into a trancelike state. A sense of amusement tugged at the corners of Dusky's lips as she realized Sam was drowsing despite the precariousness of riding on the back of a motorcycle. Though they remained on old logging and country roads, Dusky slowed her speed and avoided potholes, occasionally using a hand to steady Sam's arms around her waist. "Shake, point."

Shake sped past her. He caught a glimpse of Sam and rolled his eyes with a grin. "Nice."

Dusky gave him a shrug, careful to not dislodge Sam's head. She smirked at him. "What can I do?"

He shook his head, laughing into the mic before gunning the engine and overtaking her. Remy pulled up just enough to see what they were talking about and fell back once more, his face impassive.

Annoyance soured Dusky's good humor. Remy didn't have a problem with her interest in women and never had. His focus had always been on his nieces growing up to provide heirs and take leadership of the Lichii Ba'Cho. With Dusky's sister and father dead, Remy had increased his familial pressure on her to find a man, make a baby. *It ain't like this is Europe; this ain't a dynasty.* Her father, Ice, had realized this. The brothers, founding fathers of the once largest band of American Indian nomads, had been at odds about this since the collapse of the economy in the twenty teens. Ice had wanted the Lichii Ba'Cho to follow the cultural form of government that had existed prior to the European invasion, giving people the freedom to follow whomever they wanted without pressure. Remy clung to the dynastic view he'd learned in school. Sam shifted behind her, the motion distracting Dusky's thoughts to something more pleasant.

She pressed her hand against Sam's arms, remembering their morning. That kiss had been as electric as the first time Dusky had laid eyes on Sam. When Sam had blurted out that she thought Dusky was beautiful, Dusky hadn't been able to ignore her desire. The only thought she remembered just before Remy had interrupted them was that she deserved a kiss from those intriguing lips. *Why not? All the stories say I should get a reward for saving the damsel in distress.* She'd felt a bit of struggle from Sam, but that hadn't stopped her. A little fight could be fun in the right circumstances; if Sam really hadn't wanted it, Dusky would have backed off. She reveled in the memory, the taste and smell of Sam. *Roses, definitely roses.* It was too bad she and the *preciada* wouldn't be able to spend much time in Boise together.

After another hour of travel, Dusky glanced back at Remy. He looked haggard, the result of an old man spending hours on the road. "All right. Lunch break. Pull it over up at that clearing, Shake."

Rather than respond verbally, Shake raised a hand to indicate he'd heard her order. He slowed and pulled onto the shoulder of the logging road, shutting down his engine. Dusky pulled behind, and Remy passed them both before parking his bike. Remy straightened to work some kinks out of his back as Shake hopped off to dig into his saddlebags.

Dusky straddled her bike and patted Sam's arms. "*Preciada.*" Sam's arms unconsciously squeezed her waist in a hug, and Dusky had a sudden visualization of Sam's hands stroking her from behind, those hands reaching beneath leathers and cloth to caress her abdomen and breasts. She licked her lips at the delectable burn of arousal, regretful when Sam woke enough to pull away. *I need to get laid.* Not liking the sense of loss Sam's physical distance triggered, Dusky quickly dismounted. "Lunchtime."

Unaware of Dusky's lascivious interest, Sam stretched. "Where are we? What time is it?"

Remy answered. "Somewhere around New Meadows." He accepted a box of food from Shake.

Dusky forced herself to look away as Sam clambered off the motorcycle. She stared out over the clearing, looking up at the hazy sky. Beside her, Sam massaged her lower back. "Ouch. My fanny's going to be killing me tomorrow." Shake gave them both a box of rations, and she promptly ripped it open. "How long before we arrive in Boise?"

Dusky turned her back on Sam, refusing to allow her mind to conjure up images of massaging the soreness from Sam's muscles. When Dusky didn't respond, Shake answered. "Another four or five hours, give or take. It'll be slow going in the mountains until we get to the desert. We'll have a straight shot from there." He took a swig from his canteen.

"We're going to need gas," Remy said.

"We'll pick some up in one of the mountain towns." Dusky rubbed her face with one hand. "Probably McCall."

Sam chewed and swallowed a mouthful of food. "Then what?"

Dusky glanced over her shoulder at the *gringa*, then turned back to study the surrounding hills. "We see if Uncle Sam'll pay a reward for his missing property. Plug in for the night. Split in the morning."

"We gonna go to Ritzy's, Dusk?" Shake's eyes lit up.

What an excellent idea. Dusky turned back with a grin. "Yeah, why not?" she drawled.

Remy snorted and gave them a wry smile. "Yeah, I'll leave that to you youngsters. Me? I'll get a drink and head up to the flop. You guys can tear the town down." He raised his hand at Shake's beginning argument. "Somebody's gotta be able to post bail, you know."

Dusky thought of tearing Sam's clothes off instead. *Cool it, Holt.* While it was fun to poke fun at Sam, the fact remained that they were worlds apart. The Ba'Cho needed to get to Seattle, and Sam needed to return to her real life, a life that had nothing to do with running wild on the highways. She surreptitiously looked at Sam, who remained silent as Shake attempted to cajole Remy into partying with them at Ritzy's. *What is it about her?* Sam glanced in her direction, their eyes meeting. Dusky felt a rush of desire flow through her, noting Sam's answering flush. *Maybe I should bang her tonight, get past this.* The thought heightened her arousal, and she licked her lips. Sam swallowed, looking slightly stunned. Dusky smiled and looked away, the mood broken as she saw Remy staring at her with a raised eyebrow.

Damn it. Dusky pushed away from her bike. "Come on, let's go. The sooner we're there, the sooner we can party."

Riding pillion behind Dusky once more, Sam grasped Dusky's hips as Remy led them forward. Dusky missed the warm sensation of Sam leaning against her. *I can fix that.* She smiled as she hit the nearest rut worn into the gravel road, forcing Sam to lean close and hold tighter.

* * *

Shimizu played a solo game of racquetball at the Azteca gymnasium. Sweat dripped from him as he slammed the ball to the floor, running to intercept it when it ricocheted from the wall back at him. His phone rang, and he used a flick of his wrist to access the line, never ceasing his game. "Shimizu!"

"Yes, sir, Harrelson, sir. The new troops just arrived. Where do you want them deployed?"

The small black ball raced toward him, and he gracefully backhanded it away. "Have 'em hang out between Boise and the mountains. That has to be where the courier was headed." The ball returned and he sailed it away again with a resounding *thwock*. "Keep an eye on all roads coming out of the Rockies."

"Yes, sir. Anything else, sir?"

"You play racquetball, Harrelson?" Another approach, another hit.

Harrelson sounded mournful. *"No, sir, I don't."*

"Then you'd better learn. I'll see you at the courts next Thursday at one." Sweat ran into his eyes, and he missed the next swing, the ball bouncing furiously away.

"Yes, sir! I'll be there."

Shimizu disconnected the line and retrieved the ball.

CHAPTER TWELVE

Coming out of the Rockies, the nomads were forced to head toward civilization as they traversed the yellow, rolling hills. There were no logging roads in the desert plains, and towns were few and far enough between that side roads weren't plentiful. They skirted towns that grew progressively larger as the terrain flattened around them. Farmland began to appear, large squares of acreage in varying colors of greens and browns. The air smelled of dust, mint and onions. Traffic picked up around them—beat-up vehicles that had seen even worse days than the bikes, the incidental electric car puttering along at a measly twenty-five kilometers an hour and even a lone three-wheeled bicycle ridden by an old man wearing nothing but a G-string and sandals. He was the only person that they passed that didn't have fear, disgust or loathing on his face.

Sam watched the Ba'Cho for any response to the public denigration as slower moving vehicles pulled out of their way, the drivers glaring in anger or looking away in terror. She saw nothing. Gone were the easy chattering of Shake and the rare smiles from Remy, replaced with stone-faced countenances. Was their aloofness a defense against others' responses or an offensive maneuver to drive outsiders away? *Running with the wrong crowd again, Elias. When are you ever going to learn?* She smiled at the thought, gasping as Dusky hit a rough spot in the road, forcing Sam to compensate by holding tight.

They passed through the outskirts of Horseshoe Bend, veering west to circle the town barricade. Sam studied the concrete structure as they passed. It looked like some ancient city, standing several meters high. The razor wire strung along the top outer edge and the obvious gun placements reminded her that this was the mid-twenty-first century. A thriving shantytown had sprung up in the shadow of the wall, smelling of cooking smoke and raw sewage as they passed. She'd heard that some American cities had blockaded themselves, but this was the first she'd seen with her own eyes. The Ba'Cho didn't bother to approach any of the large gates. Instead Dusky led them across a rickety footbridge, ignoring the terrified squawk and scurry of frightened pedestrians. A mangy dog didn't appear intimidated as it chased them for a half a kilometer before tiring. Sam looked back to see it panting heavily, sides lathered. On the south side of town, they reconnected with the highway, crossing a sturdier bridge. Here the wind was just right to deliver a disgusting odor.

"Ugh!" Sam felt the tremor of a chuckle in Dusky. "What is that?"

Dusky had to call out to be heard as they picked up speed. "Dog food plant."

Sam gagged, burying her face in Dusky's shoulder. Fortunately, the air quality cleared as they left Horseshoe Bend behind them, though, hints of the stench wisped across their path from the filthy river they paralleled.

Several minutes later, Dusky pulled forward as Shake fell back. "Almost there!" Shake pointed to a sign that said "Boise 20 miles."

Sam felt a pang of regret. Frowning, she glanced back to see Shake taking the flank position, Remy pulling up to shadow Dusky. *Almost there.* Instead of relief that she'd almost finished this job, she wished it had taken longer. She toyed with the idea of using her payment to hire Dusky to drive her back to Seattle. She'd see more of the country that way. *I'd have a better chance of being arrested too. Besides, she said they have someplace to be.* Dejected, Sam wrapped her arms around Dusky's waist, not wanting to release her so soon.

She didn't realize anything was wrong until she heard the squeal of rubber on the road. She turned back to see Shake had stopped in the middle of the road, grabbing the light anti-tank weapon he had taken from the attack that had destroyed her convoy. He slid it open and placed it on his shoulder, aiming west. It happened so fast that she didn't know what he was shooting until she followed the rocket as it launched. It hit a white SUV paralleling the highway, exploding. *What?* Before her stunned mind could catch up to what she witnessed, she grasped tightly at Dusky as the bike braked and spun around.

Gunfire erupted from another SUV cresting a hill thirty meters away. Shake had barely started moving again when he was hit, the round knocking him and his bike to the ground. Remy had also stopped at the opening volley of the attack, but now turned to bellow at Dusky. Sam couldn't hear the words, but his intention was clear. He tossed his rifle to Dusky and he turned his bike to go back for their fallen comrade. Dusky caught the weapon with ease. She sighted the second vehicle and fired. Rather than the now-familiar sound of bullets, Sam heard two hollow metallic thumps as Dusky used the grenade launcher attached to the barrel of the machine gun. One bounced ineffectively off the windshield of her target, but the second blew the undercarriage and severely damaged the transmission. The SUV slowed to a smoking halt. A half dozen shock troopers poured out in full riot gear, putting up a defensive circle around the ruined vehicle.

Sam cringed behind Dusky, looking back to see that Remy had reached Shake. He looked bloody, but he had the strength and presence of mind to grab his saddlebags and straddle the bike behind Remy, holding on for all he was worth. Remy whipped about and sped back to Dusky as a third SUV came into view. It bounced as it took the rough ground at speed, ignoring the angry shock troopers on foot as it pulled into their field of fire.

Dusky tried to fire another grenade, but the mechanism jammed. "Fuck!" She handed the weapon behind her to Sam. "Hang on, *gringa!*" She hit the gas, laying down rubber, and accelerated away, Remy and Shake on her tail.

It boiled down to a matter of speed and time. The two bikes weaved back and forth to avoid being hit, throttles wide open. They pushed it until the Harleys started to protest, whining and shuddering as they flew down the road. Crouched low, clutching Dusky with one hand and awkwardly holding the lethal machine gun in the other, Sam risked a glance back. They had gained some time; the remaining car couldn't keep up on the rough ground and had to cut over to the highway. Up ahead, the Fort Boise Wall materialized before them. The corporation vehicle lurched onto the hardtop with a distant screech of rubber and sped up. There wasn't a vast difference, but she saw it gain ground. A small turret swung around, taking aim. "Here it comes!" She buried her face in Dusky's back. There was an explosion to their left, and the bike wobbled from the concussion.

Remy's bike inched up beside them. Dusky poured on the acceleration despite the growing complaint from her bike. Sam saw people gathering on the wall and movement in the twin towers bracketing the gate. *Let's hope they can tell the difference between friend and foe.* Another explosion rocked the bike, this time on the right, and Sam squeaked. As they came into range of the tower guns, a third concussion slammed them, almost driving the bike into a ditch on the side of the road. Flames from the round had come close enough to singe the hair off Sam's right arm. The mortars in the towers fired a volley. The bikes slowed down in the shadow of the wall, and Sam took the opportunity to look back. The riot car sent out a final shot that fell far short as it screeched to a halt and reversed. In seconds, it was hightailing it away, rounds bursting about them.

Dusky twisted in her seat, her hand hard against Sam's at her abdomen. "You okay?"

"Yeah, I'm good. Check on Shake." Sam released her death grip.

Setting the bike on its stand, Dusky dismounted and went to Remy's bike. Shake swore a blue streak, bleeding from a shoulder wound, his saddlebags hanging loosely in one hand. Remy had already begun applying pressure to the wound. "Looks okay, Dusk. In and out, clean as a whistle."

Dusky nodded, gripping Shake's good shoulder.

Sam heard a rumble behind her as the gates opened. A squad of ten police officers poured out, rifles ready. They spread out and covered the nomads as another man followed them out.

"Welcome to Boise, Idaho."

* * *

"Captain?" Lt. Colonel Gina Conway looked up as her aide burst through her office door.

"Radio, Colonel! There's been an attack at the North Hills Gate."

Conway wasted no time in grabbing her ear-mic from the desktop charger. The tinny sound of excited voices became louder and richer as she seated the mechanism into her ear. At the first pause in the chatter, she tapped the transmit button on the earbud. "This is Mama Bird, report!"

"Mama Bird, this is Eagle Eye. We had four civilians chased by a corporate SUV to the North Hills Gate. They were firing upon the civilians. I authorized a return salvo with mortar."

"Did you ID the SUV?" Conway stood and turned to stare out her office window. In the distance she saw the North Hills Gate. The air there seemed a little hazy, probably from firing the rounds.

"No positive ID, Mama, though it's possible they were Azteca."

Conway swore. *Damn them.* "What about the civilians? Any casualties?"

"One wounded." There was a pause, and Conway scowled at the gate, willing herself to see what was going on firsthand. Her office wasn't wired for security video feed, and she had to wait for Eagle Eye to decide what to tell her. "Three are nomads on two bikes, ma'am. The fourth says she's a courier for Canada GovMin en route to Boise on business." Another pause. "Sam Elias, carrying a Canadian passport, requesting you by name, Mama."

If anything, Conway's mood worsened. She'd read the report about the MP convoy out of Fort Lewis being fragged in eastern Washington. Sam Elias had been their cargo. "Take them into custody, bring them to HQ."

"Yes, ma'am."

Conway pulled the ear-mic out and tossed it to the desktop. *Great.*

CHAPTER THIRTEEN

As the door closed with finality, Sam continued to try to explain. "Look! I'm a courier with the GovMin of Canada, damn it! Let me speak to Gina Conway!" The resounding click of the lock angered her, and she kicked the door in frustration. Hearing a dry chuckle behind her, she turned and glared. She stood in a meeting room with several chairs circling a broad table. Shake sat on the tabletop as Remy opened his canteen, pouring water into the bullet wound. Dusky stood at the window, smiling at Sam. Furious at her apparent amusement, Sam put her hands on her hips. "What's your problem?"

Dusky's grin widened. "No problem. Just enjoying the show." She left the window, prowling toward Sam. "Tell me, *gringa*, you expected a different sort of reception in our company?" She laughed, pulling a chair from the table and offering it to Sam. "Take a load off, little girl. It'll be a while."

Little girl? Hell, I'm older than she is! Sam growled and crossed her arms over her chest, fingernails digging into her biceps. She bypassed the chair to take a stand at the window, ignoring Dusky's soft, "Suit yourself." From here Sam had a view of the Boise Wall. Thirteen meters high, two meters thick and kilometers long, it surrounded the city. The only breaks were the occasional gates like the one they had come through. Residents weren't cut off from outside—with proper credentials and references, entry was allowed. Of course, most of Sam's paperwork was in her pack somewhere in the state of Washington, and the Ba'Cho hadn't had time to apply for permission. Fortunately, Sam had an ident patch embedded in her wrist with her passport information.

Behind her, the nomads rummaged in Shake's saddlebags and their pockets, locating a sewing kit. They'd been thoroughly searched before being allowed entry into Boise, but only their weapons and vehicles had been confiscated. Remy located a flask and splashed alcohol into Shake's wound. Shake hissed, and Sam turned to watch. Dusky had prepared a needle and thread and proceeded to sew the entry wound with small, precise stitches. Unable to help herself, Sam eased closer, both fascinated and repulsed at the rustic surgery. "I take it you've done this before?"

Dusky didn't look up. "It is what it is."

Sam watched as Dusky used her teeth to cut the thread, then pull away to rethread the needle for the larger exit wound on his back. "Won't it get infected?"

"Not if we're careful." Dusky concentrated on her task. "Once we're out of here, we'll score some antibiotics just to be sure. No need to pay a ripperdoc if the bullet's not inside. Most of 'em won't report gunshots to the authorities, but I don't want to chance it. We're wanted in Kootenai County. Sometimes reward money strangles common sense."

Wanted? Sam almost asked but shied away from the question.

The minutes ticked silently by as Dusky worked on the more complicated exit damage. Eventually, she finished her task and gently patted Shake. "Congrats. Now you can show off the scars to all the women. Women love scars."

Shake grinned, wiggling his eyebrows, looking much younger than he tried to act. Remy cut in as he bandaged the wounds. "Yeah, well, don't use that as an excuse to get too many scars, boy."

Shake moved his shoulder slowly, wincing. "Don't worry, Remy. The pain ain't worth it."

Dusky used a spill of whiskey to sanitize her hands. She moved around the table. Crossing her arms over her chest, she stared silently out the window. Sam studied her stoic profile, frowning. *What kind of world do they live in where they deal death and patch up their own wounded without a second thought?* She stepped closer to Dusky, looking out to see what she saw, hoping the same point of view would help her understand.

In an offhand voice, Dusky said, "No need to go ballistic about the wait. This is SOP."

"SOP?"

"Standard Operating Procedure. Now we just hurry up and wait." Dusky rubbed her left upper arm. "Typical military behavior."

"You've had experience, I take it?"

"Yeah. Some."

Realizing that no more information was forthcoming, Sam sighed in annoyance and turned back to the window. "Locking us up is stupid. I just wish they'd get their heads out of their asses and let me complete this job." She glanced back, catching an expression of surprised speculation on Dusky's face before it slid away into a flinty countenance.

"They're coming."

Shake's words triggered a madcap rush among them, their quick movements almost obscuring the sound of booted feet marching closer. Within seconds Shake sat tilted back in a chair, idly picking his teeth with a toothpick as he balanced on the back two legs. Remy had crossed the room to lean casually against the window frame, staring out into nothing as he pulled at his beard. Dusky had disappeared from Sam's side and was now seated on the table in front of the door. Lazy lions relaxed in the room, only there on the sufferance of their pride leader. A rattling at the door drew Sam's shocked attention away from them. The door opened to reveal four armed guards crowding the hall outside.

A corporal entered the room, glancing around. "Sam Elias?"

Sam stood tall and stared down her nose at the non-com. "Yes?"

"I've been ordered to escort you to see Colonel Conway."

She glanced at the nonchalant nomads. "What about my friends?"

The corporal shrugged. "They stay here until I get different orders, ma'am."

Sam inhaled, preparing to argue the point.

"Go. We'll wait."

Holding off her irritation, she came around the table. Dusky gave her a slight nod, and Sam sighed. *Fine.* With a frown, she turned back to the corporal. "Let's go then. I haven't got all day." Stepping past him, she entered the hall, forcing the four guards there to shuffle and give her space. Flustered, the corporal followed. Two guards remained behind as they walked away, and Sam couldn't help but internally wince at the sound of the lock hitting home.

After a series of nondescript hallways, turns and branchings, they arrived at an office. The corporal nodded to the receptionist, knocked at the interior door and ushered Sam into the next room. He quietly closed the door behind her, remaining with the two guards outside. As offices went it was small. Unlike Robert Barry's office in British Columbia, no potted plant resided here and there was a window letting in afternoon sunlight. A full set of bookshelves occupied one wall and file cabinets the other. A plump gray-haired woman behind the desk stood upon her entry. Had she worn civilian clothes, she might have been mistaken for someone's grandmother. Sam caught sight of the woman's stern face. She couldn't imagine this woman standing in a cozy kitchen dishing up cookies and milk. *Yeah, maybe not a kindly grandma.* The woman held her hand out across the desk. "Ms. Elias, I'm Lt. Colonel Gina Conway." She gestured for Sam to seat herself. "I hear you've been asking for me."

Relieved to be meeting her contact, Sam allowed herself a small smile. "Yes, I have. I'm from the Canadian Government Ministry in Vancouver, British Columbia."

"And you have something for us, correct?" Conway echoed her expression, the smile softening the tense lines of her face.

Okay, maybe she can be someone's grandma. "I do. I'm carrying a terabyte of compressed data. You have the download encryption codes?"

Conway made a face. "Well, yes and no." She flipped through a file on her desk. "We've received the codes for download, but our computers are acting up."

"Acting up?" Sam frowned.

"Yes. They've been crashing with some frequency over the last two days." She looked at the courier with sympathy. "I can't authorize your download yet. I'd hate for you to be online during a crash. There's no telling what that'd do to you or the information you're carrying."

Sam sighed in disappointment. She had hoped to get this over with quickly, daydreaming of hitching a ride with Dusky back to the coast. *But they're leaving tomorrow, providing they're not under arrest.* She focused again on the colonel who had continued talking.

"…in any case. We'll set you up with a room for the time being. Of course, you have free rein in the city. We only ask that you stay fairly close during business hours, just in case our techs stabilize the system."

"What about my friends?"

"Friends?" Conway consulted the paperwork again. "You left with a platoon of Fort Lewis military. None made it in with you." She glanced up in confusion.

"No, no. There are three nomads being held right now. They picked me up during the corporation attack on the platoon. If it wasn't for them, I'd be dead."

"Oh! Nomads, well." Conway shrugged with a dismissive air. "We'll set them back outside the walls, no problem."

Sam felt a pulsing headache develop in her temples. She glared at the officer. "You're not getting it. I want my friends released and allowed free access to the city. I also want them rewarded for helping me. They've lost time, equipment and blood to get me here."

Conway's eyes narrowed. "You're not exactly in a position to be demanding anything, missy."

"And you're not exactly in a position to be denying me, either," Sam responded in the same tone. "Just because your computers are down doesn't mean you own me. And don't think that I can't find a terminal somewhere. I can trash this," she tapped her right temple, "before you even have time to blink." At loggerheads, Sam took a deep breath. *Try another tack.* "Look, what'll it hurt to allow them out for the next day? They just want to blow off some steam and leave in the morning."

Conway stared at her for long moments. Finally, she nodded her stiff neck. "You've got it." She typed upon a wireless keypad. "They'll be released within the hour, given a small sum as reward and allowed access for the night."

"Thank you!" Sam breathed with a sweet smile. "I really appreciate it!"

Conway raised a disbelieving eyebrow at the sudden innocent act but continued typing orders. "There. Done." She pushed the keypad away and stood, the move abrupt enough that Sam almost knocked her chair down as she mirrored the action. "Your 'friends' have been taken care of.

I'll have the corporal get you a base visitor ID and show you to your room."

Sam wondered if she'd put her foot in it. She thanked Conway again, noting her stiff reaction. *Too bad. Once I dump this file, I'm out of here anyway.* She allowed herself to be dismissed and picked up the corporal in the outer office. The two burly guards had already been sent packing, and Sam sighed. *Almost done.*

* * *

As soon as Sam and the goons left, Shake groaned and eased his chair back to the ground. Remy immediately went to the saddlebags, pulling out some clothing. "We need to get your arm stabilized." He ripped a shirt, fashioning a rudimentary sling.

Dusky scowled, hopping down from the table. She'd heard the lock engage but went to the door, trying the knob anyway. She put her ear to the crack, hearing nothing outside. They wouldn't need four guards to transport Sam, so some were probably posted in the hall. *I hate this.* She turned away from the door, returning to the window.

The sun had dipped lower, casting shadows across the city. From this angle she saw scrub brush and desert hills rolling into the mountainous distance, the thick wall blocking their escape. It was a matter of time before someone in authority conducted a search on their identifications and vehicle registrations. They'd soon realize that they had three fugitives in custody. No doubt Couer d'Alene officials had put out warrants for their arrest after that shit storm up north; the next place she and her family would see would be the inside of a lockup. *Damn it. I should have left her there.* That idea, though rich in self-preservation, made her scowl. What she'd said the night of the Azteca attack on Uncle Sam still held—whatever the corporations wanted, she'd deny if at all possible. They'd wanted Sam Elias dead, and Dusky had done everything in her power to thwart their aim.

"That'll be better."

"Thanks, Remy." Shake pressed his palm against his injured shoulder as he adjusted his seat. Glancing at the door, he turned his attention to Dusky. "We're fucked, huh?"

Dusky forced her dark thoughts away, needing to show confidence for their youngest member's sake. "A bit." She gave him a lopsided grin. "We've been in worse, though."

Remy picked up the thread. "Way worse. I remember that time me and Ice had to bust out of a county drunk tank. It wasn't easy, but it can be done."

"You think we're going to be sent up?"

"Don't know." Dusky used a signal for silence, casually flipping her hand as she spoke so as not to alarm anyone watching via hidden cameras or listening. Talking freely now could implicate them in any number of things and guaranteed their future incarceration. "We did almost run down their gates."

Shake nodded, gently patting his wound with the affirmative signal.

"Can't blame us for that." Remy lowered himself into a chair with a grunt. "Besides, we saved their precious courier. That's got to count for something."

"Yeah." Dusky's gaze returned to the view. "Once they let us go, we'll take I-84 to Meridian or something. Find someplace to crash for the night, see about getting you another set of wheels."

"So, no Ritzy's?"

Dusky turned to give Shake a wry grin. "Depends on if they'll let us stay within city walls. We didn't have time to apply for entry at the gate. They might take exception and kick our asses out." She watched with fondness as Shake grumbled, and looked away. He was young and wild and hadn't had time to sow any oats since the whole mess with the Aryans had gone down. "Hey." She waited for him to catch her eye. "I promise, next time we're in the area, we'll hit Ritzy's, okay?"

His sour expression eased. "Yeah, okay, Dusk. That'll be fine."

It'll have to be. While Remy started up a conversation about what he wanted to have for dinner, Dusky stared back out the window. Sam Elias was important enough to be targeted for death by Azteca; whatever she carried had to be damned important. That might give the Ba'Cho the edge if it came down to choosing whether or not to keep them imprisoned. Sam's anger at being held seemed to include the nomads, but Dusky couldn't be sure. For all she knew, Sam would be happy enough to do her job and bail, leaving the people who helped her to rot in Uncle Sam's company. A pang struck Dusky's heart, and she closed her eyes. The memory of the unrestrained kiss they'd shared rolled over her, igniting her blood. No, Sam wouldn't dump and dash. *How the hell do I know that?* Engrossed in the puzzle, she didn't hear the booted feet approaching until Remy pointed it out. Dusky turned and approached the table, leaning her hands on it and staring across it at the door as it opened. She smothered a sense of disappointment that Sam wasn't there. Instead, the corporal stood in the doorway, looking decidedly green as he faced down three hardened nomads.

He cleared his throat. "Um, you're free to go."

Dusky kept her expression neutral despite her surprise. "Our bikes and weapons?"

The non-com held out a commpad. "If you sign here, you'll get all your belongings back."

What's the catch? Dusky pushed away from the table and circled it, ignoring the corporal's cringe as she took the commpad. She scrolled through the document, noting it was a simple inventory of their possessions, with three spots for signatures or thumbprints at the bottom. There was nothing else, no clauses, no caveats. She pressed her thumb against the reader, purposely giving it a slight twist to smudge it before handing it to Remy. "Now what?"

Again the corporal cleared his throat. He held out his hand, and one of the guards gave him an envelope. "I've been authorized to give you this." Puzzled, Dusky took it and ripped it open. As she examined the contents, he continued speaking. "There's a reward for assisting Ms. Sam Elias, and twenty-four-hour authorization for the three of you to remain inside the walls."

I'll be damned. Dusky fought the grudging smile she wanted to express. *Looks like she came through for us after all.* It warmed her heart, and she wished she could see Sam to thank her. The pleasure faded in light of reality. *That won't happen.* Sam had a life in Canada and a reputation as a courier to consider. Running with a pack of Ba'Cho wasn't her fate. Even the idea of it was absurd. It was fun while it lasted, but there was no future with the *preciada*. Remy interrupted her musings as he returned the commpad to her. She looked it over to be sure Shake had also smudged his print and held the completed form out to the corporal. The envelope went into the back pocket of her leathers. "Let's go."

* * *

Ritzy's!
Open 24 hours a day!
You name it, we've got it!

The finest selection of alcohol in the country
A half-city block dance floor
Multiple levels of entertainment
Cages
Flops
Private secure parking

Join us for Happy Hour, 4pm to 8pm!

Well Drinks for 6c!
Happy Hour Menu for 8c!

Whatever your desire, Ritzy's can find it for
you!*

Ritzy's
2207 Warm Springs Ave.
Boise, Idaho 83712

*Escort services are not regulated or monitored.
Use at your own risk.

CHAPTER FOURTEEN

EXT. UPSCALE CITY DANCE CLUB - NIGHT - GROUND CAMERA ANGLE

Wet streets, popular nightclub, lights reflecting off water, dozens of men and women in stylish clothes waiting in line to enter. Camera moves in from across the street, along the queue, up to the curb beside the main entrance—nothing but blacks and blues of a city night and neon yellow and reds of blurred overhead sign.

INT. CLUB DANCE FLOOR - NIGHT

Camera moves through the crowd at eye level, catching all activity. A mass of people, well dressed, having a great time, drinking, smoking stimstics, necking, visiting, laughing.

INSERT: BAR

Back bar lit up with fluorescents, bartender and patrons dark against its brightness.

INSERT: DANCE FLOOR

Song playing upbeat tempo, crowd jumping in unison as they dance to the beat.

BACK TO SCENE

Camera passes bar, threads through dance floor, making for

INSERT: DOOR

Sexy WOMAN lounging beside back room door, an Augment with feline facial structures and delicate whiskers.

BACK TO SCENE

Nearing the door, focus on the woman. She smiles at the camera, turns away, revealing a TIGER tattooed across her bare back. She raises a finger, crooks it at the camera with a knowing smile and opens the door.

INSERT: CLOSE UP, TATTOO

The tiger isn't stationary. It moves independent of her muscles and skin as light from the room beyond strikes it. The tiger turns its head, looks directly at the camera and opens it mouth to growl silently at the watcher.

NARRATOR (V.O.)
Neurotatts. Electrical molecular inks for the discerning collector.

WHITE OUT

Tiger eyes fade back onto the screen as the NARRATOR speaks.

NARRATOR (V.O.)
Why settle for a static image?

TIGER
(Low, deep growl)

END

* * *

Shimizu tried not to fidget. He'd been forced to attend a late lunch for the regionals and deputies and vice presidents and ad nauseum of the Azteca Corporation. Some of these bigwigs had flown in to Hermiston, Oregon, for this charade. A real time get-together, it meant there was no way to work through the tedious meal without screwing his chances for promotion. He pretended enthusiasm for the president of some obscure department, the idiot standing to a round of polite applause for his turn at the podium. Shimizu's finger tapped mindlessly on the rim of his plate.

"Mr. Shimizu?" A waiter held out a silver tray, an archaic piece of paper prominently displayed upon it.

Snatching the old-fashioned message with a smothered sense of glee, Shimizu thanked the servant and waved him away. He opened the note, quickly scanning its contents. His pleasure with the distraction faded. His staff knew better than to interrupt these quarterly shindigs without good cause and, though the note was generic enough to not tip off any executives who intercepted it, dread spiked his heart rate. He refolded the note and tucked it into his pocket. With minimal fuss, he whispered apologies to his immediate neighbors for the interruption and made his way out of the company banquet hall. Out in the foyer, he flicked his wrist, accessing his phone line. Dialing quickly, he activated the subvocal routines. He wouldn't need to speak aloud to be understood over the line. Business being as cutthroat as it was, one never knew when another executive would eavesdrop for intel to destroy his or her competition.

"Harrelson."

"Shimizu. What do you have?"

"Some good, some bad, sir."

He sounded fearful, and Shimizu hoped his growl didn't come through the line. Maybe mentoring Harrelson wasn't such a diesel idea if he couldn't mask his emotions over a comm line. "What's the bad?"

"We were unable to appropriate the original courier, sir. She made it into Boise before our team could overtake her."

He pondered Harrelson's use of the word "original." "No survivors again?" When the hell did it become so tough to find and kill a Canadian civilian? He reminded himself to send a nasty email to the Regional Director of Armed Forces.

"Most of the operatives involved in this confrontation survived. Only twelve casualties."

"Well, demote the rest of them." He chewed his lip. "What's the good news?"

Harrelson's voice lightened. Shimizu even heard the smile. *"We picked up a different Canadian courier, sir, this one heading for Boise as well."*

Two of them? Why two? "Where'd this courier originate?"

"Edmonton, Alberta, sir."

Shimizu digested that databit, eyes moving back and forth as he considered his options. Two couriers could mean twice the data being transported, or it could be that one held the encryption code for the other. He chewed his lip, pacing. "Drain the courier, let's see what GovMin's doing with Uncle Sam."

"*Yes, sir.*"

"Harrelson?"

"*Sir?*"

"Not a bad job, boy. You're due for a promotion soon?"

There was a startled hesitation before Harrelson sputtered. "*Yes, sir! My review is in forty days.*"

"Excellent. I'll put in a good word for you." Shimizu disconnected the line despite the continued gushing of gratitude from his aide. *Or not.* Catching sight of himself in a decorative mirror, he focused on his appearance, adjusting the collar of his jumpsuit and twitching his dark hair into place. *What are you up to, GovMin?* The mirror didn't answer, and he reluctantly returned to the banquet hall to finish lunch.

* * *

As the elevator descended, the bass sound from the music in the discotheque swelled. Shake's grin became toothy as the doors opened onto the main lobby. Dusky couldn't help but answer it with one of her own as her anticipation grew. Only Remy winced at the volume. He stuck a finger in his ear as they walked past the front desk where they'd checked into their rooms and to the double doors leading into Ritzy's Club. Despite the early hour—five in the evening—all three ground-level bars were crowded, though not many patrons had spilled over to take possession of the plentiful tables. Music rolled over them, and Dusky automatically scanned for the exits and promising fields of fire. There were two floors of balcony above them and cages for dancers on all levels.

Shake had donned traditional leather after his shower for his first foray into a big city establishment like Ritzy's.

He wore tan leggings, breechclout, soft boots and little else except the sling holding his wounded arm in place. "I'm going to get us drinks."

Remy waved him off, seemingly happy to let him fight the press for alcohol. He leaned close to Dusky, yelling to be heard over the music. "Where do you want to sit?"

She looked up to the third floor. "Let's go up there. Less active and a good view of things." He nodded and stumped toward the nearest set of stairs. Dusky watched him fondly for a moment before finding Shake to let them know where they'd be. When she got upstairs, she joined Remy at a tall cabaret table. The music wasn't quite as thunderous here, and they discussed what was on the menu flimsy sitting atop their table. Each balcony level had its own bar and staff, so there'd be no wait for service.

Shake arrived and set drinks in front of them. "I know you like Sapporo, Remy, but they didn't have any."

"It is what it is." Remy sneered at the bottle placed before him. "Piss water."

Dusky chuckled. She tossed back a shot of whiskey and followed it with a long swallow from a similar beer bottle. "There's ways around that." She nudged her empty shot glass to the center of the table.

Remy snorted. "Maybe if I was forty years younger and had the constitution of a teenager."

Shake pushed a stool close to the railing and watched the dance floor below. He glanced over at his comrades. "Thanks, Dusky. This is frigid."

She raised her bottle to him as a waitress arrived to take their order. Once she was gone, Dusky returned her attention to Shake. "Just count yourself lucky that Sam got us passage. We could just as easily be sitting in county right now."

Rolling his eyes, Shake made a face. "She sweats you. Of course she'd try to see you taken care of."

Dusky didn't argue his point but also didn't accept it, either. Especially not with Remy staring at her again. *So what?*

She's gone and good riddance. They nattered on about nothing much in general, passing time until their food arrived with a fresh round of drinks. The money that Uncle Sam had given them would see them through the night and leave a bit left over to purchase a used bike for Shake. One of the first things Dusky had done upon checking into her room was to find local motorcycle sales listed on the flimsies. There were three Harleys on the market from private owners in the area and one dealership that had used bikes. Once Shake had wheels, they'd blow town and never come back.

A woman strolled past on her way to the bar, disrupting Dusky's mental plans. Her spiky platinum hair looked mussed as if she'd just crawled out of a well-used bed. Dusky licked her lips as the woman stopped to flirt with someone at another table. Despite a generally slender figure, the woman had an ample bosom. *A girl could get buried in those.* The woman flashed a smile, revealing slight dimples, and Dusky smirked in response. *Oh, yeah.*

"Can I get you another round?"

The interruption startled Dusky, and she straightened from her lustful slouch to look at a waitress.

"Naw, that's plenty for me. I'm heading upstairs." Remy shoved his plates and empty bottle in the waitress's direction, standing. The waitress nodded, taking the dishes before she left.

"Aw, c'mon, Remy." Shake tossed his napkin onto his plate. "Hang out a little longer."

"Nope. This place is giving me a headache." He rubbed the back of his neck. "I'm going to order a beer through room service and soak in a hot bath with the vids."

Dusky grinned. Whenever they stayed in civilization her uncle insisted on long soak baths. She couldn't see the point of them, preferring showers to total immersion. "See you in the morning, Remy."

"Yep." He reached out and ran his knuckle along her cheek. "Don't get into too much trouble. The law will run your idents if you get busted, and it'll be a bitch breaking you out."

"We won't. Promise." She watched him as he walked away, heading for a dark alcove with an elevator. As soon as he was out of sight, she turned to Shake. "You heard the man. Behave yourself." At his crestfallen expression, she smirked. "At least a little."

Shake laughed. "Yes, ma'am." He looked over the railing. "I'm going to go down there. You'll be okay?"

His sudden concern for her was endearing. "I'll be fine." She nodded her head at the blond who had made it to the bar. "I think I have some entertainment to line up."

He followed her gaze and laughed. "Be back in a bit."

Her full attention on the woman, she barely gave Shake a nod of acknowledgment as he left the table. Slipping from her stool, she strolled toward the bar with her empty shot glass. "Can I get another?" She set the glass down in front of the woman. "And I'll pay for whatever she's having."

The woman turned, a smile on her face as she regarded Dusky with a speculative gleam. "Whiskey sour. Straight."

Dusky gave her an appraising look. "I hope that's all that's straight." The remark earned her a delighted laugh.

The woman's eyes were hazel, right now showing a hint of green-brown as she smiled. "I don't like labels."

That told Dusky everything she needed to know. "I'm Dusky."

"Hannah." She smiled, offering her hand in official greeting.

Dusky took it, bringing the palm up to her mouth. She kissed the soft skin, ignoring the florid fake nails, and nipped the meaty flesh beneath Hannah's thumb. "It's a pleasure to meet you." Their drinks appeared. Dusky released Hannah to pay for them, pleased when the hand slid to the back of her shoulder and along her back to rest at the base of her spine. "Care to join me, Hannah?"

"I would love to, Dusky."

She led Hannah back to her table, knowing that the woman was probably a paid escort. Even if she wasn't, Hannah would stay long enough to enjoy the funds Uncle Sam had been so kind as to give the Ba'Cho and maybe spend a passionate night in Dusky's bed. Dusky's gaze shied away from the wrong color eyes and the too-blond hair, preferring to focus on Hannah's ample attributes. *Sam's gone and good riddance.*

CHAPTER FIFTEEN

After the meeting ended with Lt. Colonel Conway, Sam played hell trying to relocate the room where she and the Lichii Ba'Cho had been held. The corporal had refused to take her, dropping her off at her temporary quarters and leaving her there. By the time Sam had found the meeting room, it was empty but for a few blood and whiskey stains on the table where Shake's surgery had taken place. She slowly retraced her steps, saddened she hadn't gotten the chance to thank them for their help.

Back at her assigned quarters, she took the time to look around. The place was small but well appointed with a sitting room, a bedroom and—*Lord, have mercy!*—a shower. In moments she was naked and hopping into it. She luxuriated in the warm flow of water, lathering up with government-issue soap. After rinsing, she leaned her hands against the shower walls and let the water cascade over her. As the water turned colder, she shut it off and stepped out, toweling herself dry.

She returned to the bedroom with the towel wrapped around her body and investigated her clothing. The skivvies were a goner, but her shoes could be cleaned. She sniffed at her jumpsuit and wrinkled her nose. During the last two days the 'suit had been completely ruined. Bloodstains from the Humvee crash stiffened the material, enriching the smell of sweaty fear. With the addition of road grime and the acrid odor of incendiary rounds, it was a pungent cocktail. *Now what?* She couldn't very well run around the base in a towel. To her surprise she discovered several olive drab jumpsuits hanging inside the closet. Upon closer inspection, she found one that looked about the right size. She glanced at the door. *Will I get in trouble for wearing this outside?* She examined the clothing again, noting no nametag or insignias on the shoulders or sleeves. She promised herself it wouldn't be for long as the towel hit the floor. *I'll pick something up at the first shop I see.*

Dressed, she dug through the pockets of her old 'suit. A small gold keychain with three keys on it, a lighter, a receipt for the trashed 'suit, her credstic, and a small, round disc holder for her earring. Add her freshly minted base visitor ID to the pile, and she had a pitiful collection. She hadn't owned much to begin with, and now it was even less. *Maybe I should swing back and see if anything got left behind.* The memory of the blood and smoke and bodies made her shiver. She set that idea aside. The last thing she wanted to do was to return to that place.

Forcing her memories away, Sam tossed the credstic into the air and caught it. *Time for a new set of rags.* She transferred the items to her olive drab 'suit and headed out the door. It was early evening, and food was a priority. Besides, a night in an American city? Even if she wasn't in fabled Seattle, she couldn't pass up the opportunity.

* * *

The night was young, the sun still in the sky on this mid-May evening. Sam strolled the sidewalk with a smile, wearing a simple black strap dress that came down to her mid-thighs and a new pair of shoes. A golden belt glittered at her waist with a small pouch holding the entirety of her possessions. She'd made arrangements at the clothing store for her borrowed jumpsuit to be returned to the base. Traffic had picked up as time passed, a series of tricked-out combustion vehicles passing her as they showed off paint jobs and wild modifications. At first the multitude confused her. It took nearly a half hour before she realized she was seeing the same vehicles pass her again and again. *They're cruising!* She gave a delighted laugh as a lurid purple Ford Niño slowly pulled past bearing a turbo supercharger and an obscenely long system of exhaust pipes running out the tail end. *Who knew American cruising would still be happening a hundred years later?* She wondered if this was a nostalgic resurgence like the white ink tattoos that had become the rage a few years ago.

As the shadows grew longer, the streetlights and neon lit up, beckoning people into various establishments. Sam followed the path of the cars, drifting slowly out of the immediate downtown area. She rounded a corner and saw a six-story warehouse that seemed to be a popular destination. A vast parking lot was the turnaround of choice for the cruisers as they pulled in, around and returned the way they'd arrived. From the looks of the warehouse, the peeled and flaking paint job hadn't been refreshed in fifty years as it unashamedly revealed its original brickwork. Graffiti covered the lower walls. It didn't look like the owners gave a damn about the defacement, perhaps even encouraging it. The first three floors of windows had been boarded up and painted over, and a huge neon sign blinked above the main entry.

RITZY'S!

This is what Shake was talking about. Sam walked closer, the air throbbing with music as she neared. The entrance had once been a loading dock and looked quite active for such an early hour. With a hopeful smile and a shrug, she got in line.

"Active" was an understatement of epic proportions. Once she was inside, it felt like the entire population of Boise had beat her there. She couldn't imagine what it would be like when the sun had set and the Saturday night parties began in earnest. She pushed her way through the press, delighted by her surroundings. Bright lights flashed in her eyes, and she felt the music thunder against her sternum. Smoke machines colored the air with hints of herbal scents. Cigarette and stimstic smoke added to the heady aroma, mixing with the odors of more potent and illegal narcotics. The patrons wore both garish and somber colors, showing off cybernetics and tattoos sparkling incandescent in old-fashioned black lights and displaying hairstyles of varying lengths and unnatural hues. The wait staff, male and female, wore clear plastic swimsuits, leaving nothing to the imagination. Though Sam had been in similar establishments in her country, she realized that the American equivalent held a rougher, harder and darker edge to it, exactly like the vids portrayed.

She clutched the free drink she'd been given, making for the stairs on the other side of the dance floor. There were two levels of balconies above. Perhaps she'd be able to spot the Ba'Cho in this mass of humanity from a higher vantage point. She paused on the first balcony long enough to confirm her quarry wasn't there before proceeding higher. At the top, she moved away from the stairs and leaned against the railing, peering down at the dance floor. She watched people jump in time with the music, reminded of the dance Dusky had performed. That one had been much more graceful and deadly. Another memory blotted it out, one of warm lips against hers, tongue questing. She closed her eyes with a shiver. *I'm not here for that.* Opening her eyes again, she took a swallow of her drink, reminding herself that she only wanted to tell the nomads thank you and good-bye. *Yeah, you keep telling yourself that, Elias.* With a grimace, she drained her glass.

Not sighting any of the Ba'Cho below—which honestly was tantamount to looking for the proverbial needle in a haystack—Sam turned to check out this level. It was less frenetic than the one below and seemed darker as most the lights from the ceiling focused on the activity downstairs. Hanging from the ceiling were several cages at both eye level and below her. At first glance, she thought a couple was dancing in one of them. Upon closer inspection, she discovered they were doing something much more intimate. She felt her skin flush as she pushed away from the railing, averting her gaze. As she neared a shadowed corner, the flash of someone lighting a stimstic caught her eye.

Glasses and bottles littered a tall cabaret table, a light recessed in the ceiling providing dim illumination. Four barstools had been pulled around the table, and two were occupied. One was a pale woman wearing thigh-high boots, a tiny clinging skirt and an almost nonexistent tube top across her ample bosom. Her platinum hair spiked out in a carefully controlled haphazard mess, and a dragon tattoo spiraled down her left arm, from shoulder to wrist, the golden hues glowing in the available light. She held the stimstic, inhaling the euphoric smoke and laughing at something her companion said. It was her partner that drew Sam's complete attention. Dusky had exchanged her riding leathers for a pair of dark pants and a white sleeveless shirt that was unbuttoned to her navel. Her long hair had been freed from its braid, cascading across her shoulders in long, luxurious waves. Her tan arms contrasted against the blond's pale skin where she had wrapped herself around the woman. As Sam watched, Dusky nibbled on her friend's throat, her right hand blatantly kneading the woman's breast through her clothing. The woman didn't protest, arching her long neck to allow Dusky easier access and taking another jaded drag off the stimstic.

Sam froze, emotions seething within her. It took several seconds for her to sort through them—shock at Dusky's disregard for public exhibition; excitement and desire, wanting to take the blond's place; anger for even considering such a flagrant display herself; and a stab of jealousy so strong that it unnerved her. The morass too much to deal with, Sam whirled around, grasping the railing for support as she stared at the dance floor. She felt the heat of arousal mixing with embarrassment as she tried to stop her erratic heartbeat. *I have to get out of here!* She gulped air, willing herself to stop hyperventilating. This wasn't what she had expected, wasn't what she had wanted. *What did you want?* Her breathing normalized, she steeled herself. If she could get back downstairs, she could leave without Dusky ever being the wiser. *Don't turn around.* Despite her admonition, she snuck a peek over her shoulder as she headed for the stairs. Dusky's hand had slipped down and was effortlessly sliding beneath her companion's too-short skirt. A flash of anger pulsed in Sam's chest. *Like she can see past that set of knockers anyway.* Someone bumped into her, grabbing her, and her heart raced once more.

"Hey, *gringa!*" Shake wrapped his good arm around Sam's waist. He'd changed clothes as well and his shoulder sported proper bandages now. His appraisal was frank and interested. "You looking good enough to eat. C'mon! Party's over here." He steered his reluctant package toward the table she'd tried to avoid. Unable to deflect the inevitable, Sam steeled herself as she was briskly taken toward the two necking women. She was glad for the darkness hiding her blazing skin. As soon as they were within hailing distance, Shake hollered, "Dusky! Look who came to chip in with us!"

Dusky, lips currently occupied with the blond's, opened her eyes to have a look. She broke off the kiss, and a sultry smile crossed her lips. "*Gringa.* It's good to see you. This is Hannah." Ignoring Hannah's grimace at the interruption, Dusky plucked the stimstic from her hand and took a puff.

Shake eyed Hannah at the table. "Whaddya say, Dusk? Wanna trade?"

"Trade?" Hannah glared. With a wicked lopsided grin, Dusky nodded to Shake. He deposited Sam on a stool next to Dusky. Coming around the table, he attempted to slide his arm around Hannah's waist. She batted him away. "What the hell! I'm not a piece of meat. What if I don't want to go with the kid?"

A dangerous glint entered Dusky's eyes, one that caused Sam's heart to stammer in her chest as she recognized it. She'd seen the same expression when Dusky had disarmed her at the corporation attack. "Then you chip out before you get flatlined."

Hannah blinked, apparently surprised to be threatened. She scowled at Dusky, gauging the truth of her statement. With a blustery sigh, she rolled her eyes and hopped off the stool. "Fine." She draped her arm around Shake's shoulder, her fingers sliding up to tease the skin behind his ear. "What he doesn't have in staying power, he'll make up for in energy."

The tension eased as Shake led Hannah away. "Hey, *querida*. Did you hear about the corps firefight on the wall today?" He steered her toward the stairs.

Dusky watched them go with a smirk before bringing her attention to Sam. The light caught the silver of her cyberoptics, making her left eye spark. She regarded Sam. "Nice dress."

Sam smoothed a wrinkle in the fabric at her thigh. "Um...thanks." Dusky's nearness intoxicated her, and she fought for some emotional control. Still appalled at Hannah's treatment, she nevertheless recognized a sliver of satisfaction that the woman had been sent packing. That coupled with her voyeuristic arousal sapped her confidence. Rather than meet Dusky's eyes, she glanced around this level. "Where's Remy?" When her gaze darted back, she knew her discomfort wasn't lost on Dusky.

Grinning, Dusky reached for her drink. "Upstairs. One beer and he unplugged. He prefers soaking in a bathtub." She drained her glass and waved for a waitress. Glancing at the empty glass still clutched in Sam's hand. "What are you drinking?"

"Um...what?" Dusky's fingers brushed Sam's as the glass was pulled away from her. She shivered at the lingering touch and gulped. "Uh…I dunno. Just something…" She blew out a breath, shaking her head. *God, you're a zero.* Forging onward, she succumbed to her need to explain. "It was something they handed out at the entrance."

Dusky nodded and gave the waitress their order. She took another hit off the stimstic, a glass cylinder packed with a mild dose of stimulant. The smoke residue drifted across the table, and she offered it to Sam. "Want some?"

Already nervous, the last thing Sam wanted was to indulge, whether this particular brand was legal or not. Getting busted under the influence of illegal substances in a foreign country while still on a job would professionally destroy her. She gave a little shake of her head.

Not to be denied, Dusky leaned closer. Sam swallowed. "It's just a stimulant, nothing bad. Takes the edge off, that's all." When Sam refused a second time, Dusky lowered her chin and stared at her with a no-nonsense expression. "Remember what I said last night?"

"You're mine now." The memory brought up a combination of confusion and annoyance. Sam glared back.

Dusky held out the stimstic. "That's an order, *gringa*."

Sam debated. She'd had her share of stimulants during her wild, misspent youth, so it wasn't as if she hadn't any experience. *You make it sound like you're ancient, Elias.* She realized it wasn't that she had an aversion to the drug use; it was the presence of the woman offering that put up her internal blocks. The irritation deepened, a part of her refusing to back down from the challenge in the direct gaze leveled at her. With a practiced air, she took the stimstic from Dusky's hand and inhaled the smoke. Piqued, she purposely exhaled it into Dusky's face, ignoring the slow grin that developed there. For good measure, she had another puff before returning it to Dusky's hand. Dusky sat back, an expression of grudging acceptance on her face. *Score one for the home team.* The drug began to hit Sam's system as the lights and colors sharpened around her.

The waitress returned, and Dusky paid for the drinks. "So, why are you here, *gringa*?"

Shrugging, her hands once again occupied with a glass, Sam visually avoided Dusky, watching the passing people as more ventured to the third floor for seating. "Just out looking around. I remembered you and Shake talked about this place. When I saw it, I thought I'd see if I could find you." She felt Dusky shift beside her.

Smothering the stimstic on the tabletop, Dusky took a sip of her drink. "You found me. Now what?"

"Now…" Sam chewed the inside of her mouth. *Now what?* "I wanted to thank you for getting me here. When I got back to the conference room you had already left, and I didn't get the chance." She drained her glass and set it down, barely tasting the alcohol. This wasn't about a thank-you, and she knew it. *You want her and you're too much of a chickenshit to say anything.* The vision of Dusky with Hannah passed through her mind. *I want more than that.*

Dusky nodded. "I see." She looked away, watching the crowd, then back at Sam.

Unable to meet her gaze, Sam turned away. She felt fingers grasp her chin, turning her head toward Dusky. Warm lips brushed hers, and she closed her eyes, allowing herself to feel the exhilaration of arousal. Dusky demanded entry as she had that morning, and Sam readily granted it. Dusky tasted of smoke and sage and beer, and an urgency grew between them that hadn't been present that morning. Blindly, Sam rested her fingers on the hand at her chin, her fingers feeling the wild pulse at the delicate wrist. *I caused that.* Encouraged by the rapid heartbeat, she stepped up their kiss, devouring Dusky's mouth. Dusky retreated, sucking Sam's tongue. Sam moaned deep in her throat as she explored this new haven.

The hand at her chin disappeared. Not to be denied, Sam transferred both of hers to the dark mane of Dusky's hair, feeling its thick silkiness run through her fingers. Her mouth continued to move on Dusky's. Strong hands settled on her waist, and there was a sharp thrill of movement. Then she sat across Dusky's lap, the heat of her body pressing against Sam's right side. She had a fleeting panicked thought that they were in a public place and should stop. Dusky countered it by breaking off their kiss, her lips and teeth gliding across the fragile skin of Sam's throat. All mental activity ceased; Sam only felt the warm, wet mouth along her skin. She extended her right arm across Dusky's shoulders, using it to stabilize herself as she continued to guide Dusky's head with her other hand. She felt naughty and sexy, welcoming the desire radiating off Dusky, meeting it with her own as her body burned. She felt a hand at her waist, caressing the shiny texture of her dress, making it move against her skin— slippery and sliding, erotic. Teeth and lips blazed a trail to her tender earlobe, and Dusky's questing hand slid over her breast, teasing the nipple through the thin material. Sam gasped, arching into the cupped hand, moaning when Dusky brought her nipple to attention with a series of light pinches.

Dusky traced Sam's ear with her tongue. She breathed warm air into it, causing Sam to tremble. "You taste very good, *preciada*."

The low voice did wonders with Sam's hunger. Dusky's voice in her ear sent a sharp throb of arousal down her body, a gush of wetness following in its wake. Her body was on fire and she couldn't catch her breath. Tilting her head, Sam licked a path along Dusky's jawline until she reached the ear. She sucked Dusky's lobe into her mouth and gently bit down, reveling in the sighing moan she received. Dusky's hand on her breast hadn't ceased its movement, kneading and pinching, fanning the flames of her excitement. As entrancing as Dusky's touch was, Sam wanted to hear more of her voice. She abandoned the back of Dusky's head, drawing her hand down her neck and slipping inside the white shirt conveniently opened to the waist. She felt Dusky's abdomen muscles tense and shiver under her touch, and she smiled, nipping again at the earlobe between her teeth. She brought her hand up to cup Dusky's breast under the cloth, loving the feel of warm skin as her thumb brushed across the already erect nipple. She should have known better than to make that sort of challenge. Dusky growled, a thoroughly sensual sound that did wonders to Sam's rampaging libido, and accepted. She renewed her attack on Sam's throat with voracious appetite. Sam didn't quite panic as deft fingers slid the strap off of her shoulder. Dusky's mouth followed the path of collarbone to shoulder. She didn't stop. From there, she moved south, biting firmly into the chest muscle above Sam's collar. Her callused palm stroked Sam's length, moving with excruciating slowness up the outside of Sam's thigh, slipping beneath the hem that had ridden up her leg.

A throat cleared nearby. "Sorry to interrupt."

Dusky growled in frustration. She raised her head to glare at Shake. "This had better be good."

Shame rushed through Sam at her wanton behavior. *God, what is wrong with me?* She shifted in Dusky's lap, trying to disengage as much as possible. Dusky clamped her hand down on Sam's upper arm, forcing Sam's hand to remain upon her breast. Startled, Sam froze in place.

Despite the threat in Dusky's voice, Shake smirked. "It's good, Dusk." He still had Hannah with him, who glared daggers at Sam. Next to them stood a very large man. "You remember Delva?"

Sam squinted up at the big man. He stood two inches taller than Shake and was seventy pounds heavier, all of it muscle. He wore black silk pants and a white tank top that clung to his muscular frame. His face was clean-shaven and his dark hair was in a military buzzcut. His beefy upper arms had thick scar tissue in the shape of the army private first class rank, and on the skin outside his right eye were two tiny red feather tattoos exactly like Shake's.

Dusky grinned and reached out a hand, taking the man's forearm. "Delva! You stationed here, you dawg?"

The large man smiled back, firmly gripping her arm. "Yep. Got here six months ago." He took one of the stools and settled down. "One more year and ETS, End of Term Service. No more Army."

Shake and Hannah joined them, the woman looking haughty as she ignored Dusky and Sam. Shake snagged a drink from a passing waiter and sucked it down before wrapping his good arm around Hannah once again. Her jealousy delighted him as she moved closer to nuzzle his ear in an obvious attempt to upset Dusky.

Sam didn't know whether to laugh or cry at the woman's attempts. She remained silent, listening to the three Lichii Ba'Cho catch up with one another. Dusky's fingers idly grazed her upper arm, playing with the still hanging dress strap, her touch rekindling Sam's arousal. Either the stimulant or her rampant arousal had overtaken her common sense, or she was emboldened by the shadows and the noise. Sam brushed her thumb against Dusky's nipple, moving in slow, circular motions. She felt a thrill of pleasure at the sensual smile she received in reward.

Eventually the conversation turned solemn. "Heard about the Aryan thing on the news. Shake mentioned something?" Delva trailed off, question in his tone.

Dusky looked down. From her vantage point, Sam saw her marshaling her emotions and wondered why. "All dead. Only us and Remy made it through."

Sam stared. *Oh, my God!* She'd had no idea. She glanced at the others, seeing a flash of pain and anger shoot through Delva's eyes. Shake stared at the tabletop, and Dusky's flinty expression held a hint of brittle fragility. *Is that why there aren't any others with them?* She released Dusky's breast, sliding her hand around her waist in comfort.

Delva ground his teeth. "The Aryans?"

"Gone for good. We picked up the last one five days ago." Dusky leaned forward slightly, eyes boring into the man's. "Your family died on their feet, fighting. Your brother killed six of them before they could bring him down." She swallowed. "When you get out, I have a scalp for you—the one who took your mother's life is no more."

Delva's mother? There were women and children involved? Sam tried to remember if she'd ever heard of an American nomad gang that consisted of families. The grisly turn of the conversation overrode her desire to comfort Dusky. Sudden bloody images of nomadic warriors screaming battle cries and killing indiscriminately filled her vision. She shuddered. Dusky hugged her in response, and Sam looked up into an amused gaze.

Delva nodded. "Thanks, Dusk. I'm just sorry I couldn't have flatlined him myself." He took a long swig from his glass and looked at Sam. "Is that the *gringa* I heard you brought in?"

"Yes, it is." Dusky smiled like an indulgent parent. Her right hand reached up to brush Sam's blond hair from her temple and tuck it behind one ear. She ran her thumb over the delicate skin, and Sam shivered at the touch, trying to hold on to the spark of anger that had arisen at Dusky's possessive actions. "She's pretty, isn't she?"

Delva nodded in agreement and glanced at Shake, eyes flicking to Hannah running her black painted nails up and down Shake's chest.

Catching the look, Shake frowned, regretful. He nodded. "*Querida*, chip out. Family business." Within seconds, Hannah was shoved off her stool and away from the table. "Maybe later, sweetcheeks." Shake leered.

Hannah stared at them before marching off in a huff. Delva grinned and shook his head. Sam wondered if she was going to be as unceremoniously dumped too, but Dusky kept her in a firm grip. Sam frowned.

Delva nudged a chin at Sam. "They want her flatlined."

"Kinda figured." Shake nodded. "Azteca lost a lot of manpower trying to get her."

"No," Delva said. "Uncle Sam wants her dead."

Sam gaped. *That's ridiculous.* Dusky snarled, and she shrank away from the apparent anger. Considering their intimacy, it wasn't an easy prospect.

Delva continued. "Whatever she's carrying, they don't want it."

"Of course, they do." Sam broke into the conversation. "GovMin in Canada sent the file." She looked at the speechless nomads, realizing she may have stuck her foot in it. "I mean…What's the point of sending me here if it's just to be killed? It doesn't make sense." She scanned the table. The Ba'Cho stared for a beat longer, acting amazed that she spoke for herself. A slow burn of anger flashed in her chest, and she glared back. *I am not an idiot!*

Dusky was first to look away. "She's right. What's the point of hiring her, paying her and then rewarding us for getting her here?"

Scrubbing at his face, Delva shrugged. "I don't know. Uncle Sam moves in mysterious ways. You know that, Dusk." He indicated her cyberoptic implant, piquing Sam's curiosity. "They've been looking all over the post for her for over an hour. It's only a matter of time before they send soldiers through the city."

Sam set aside her interest in Dusky's military past and shook her head. "No, that can't be right. I spoke with my contact already." She looked at Dusky, still shaking her head. "Colonel Conway knew I was coming and where I was from. They have my download codes. She said she had no problem with me leaving post so long as I hung around during business hours. It's a done deal as soon as I download."

"*Preciada*, you still have the file?" Dusky asked in amazement.

"Yes. She said their computers were buggy and crashing. They didn't want to risk the data in a crash during download…" She trailed off at movement across the table.

Delva was shaking his head no. "We haven't had any crashes, *gringa*. Not for the six months I've been here. And I work IT."

CHAPTER SIXTEEN

Shimizu stopped, interrupted by the insistent buzzing of his phone line. "Shimizu!"

"*Sir, sorry to bother you, sir, but you said…*"

"I know what I said, Harrelson. What have you got?" He sat up in bed, red silk sheets pulling away from the prostitute beside him.

"*The courier, sir, the second one. We've drained the data from the processor. It's really weird stuff, sir.*"

"Any ideas?" The woman stirred, stretching deliciously against the silk ties that held her hands and his eyes watched her every move.

"*The lab seems to think that it's some sort of viral blocking program.*" Harrelson sounded doubtful. "*But it's set up for a virus nobody's seen before.*"

Shimizu scowled, his hand unconsciously stroking his erection. "The program or the virus?"

"*The virus, sir. As far as we know, it doesn't exist.*"

He frowned, thinking over the problem. "Is it possible to extrapolate from the program what the virus does?"

"*I don't know, sir. I'll get the lab working on it now.*"

"Good. Let me know as soon as you find out anything. And I want a full report on my desk by morning."

"*Ye—*"

Shimizu traced the path of a red welt on the prostitute's back. He listened to her seductive moan with a smile. *All work and no play.*

* * *

The nomads crowded into Dusky's room, Sam in tow. With Delva's bulk, the room seemed much smaller. Dusky sent Shake to collect Remy, while Sam curled up at the head of the bed. Delva sat at the foot of it. Dusky stared out the floor-to-ceiling window at the city below. It was beginning to move into late evening. The sun sat on the horizon, casting long shadows, and the denizens of the night had begun to roust themselves. Looking down at the loading dock, she watched the crowd of people awaiting entry expand.

How many were soldiers? How many were off-duty *malandros* seeking Sam's blood? She glanced over at Sam, seeing those brilliant blue eyes swimming in a pallid face. Dusky gave her a reassuring grin and turned back to the window, smile fading. *And what has this to do with the Lichii Ba'Cho? Nothing.* She closed her eyes when she heard the door open. Remy entered with Shake. *I am not looking forward to this.* Trying to convince elders of anything was beyond difficult. Considering the target was an outsider, convincing Remy would be harder. Dusky remained silent as her uncle and Delva greeted each other with enthusiasm. The bed creaked as the older man sat down beside him. Staying silent, Dusky waited until the talk had stopped. Instinctively, she knew when all eyes were upon her. Without turning, she said, "Tell him, Delva."

Delva cleared his throat. "Uncle Sam's put a hit out on the *gringa*. They want her dead. It's just a matter of time before they stop searching the base and spread out over the city."

"So?" Remy sounded unimpressed.

"*Preciada*."

"I was hired by Canada GovMin to deliver this file to Uncle Sam. They told me they couldn't download it yet, that the computer system was buggy." Sam paused, her words hesitant. "But Delva says that there's nothing wrong with the computers."

Her words didn't improve Remy's opinion. "I repeat… So?"

"So." Dusky turned around and faced her family, her friends, arms crossed in front of her chest. "I'm going to get her out of the city."

Shake rolled his eyes and leaned heavily against the door. Sam ogled her. Delva raised a disbelieving eyebrow, mouth dropping open. He, of all of them, would have a firm understanding of city security. *There's got to be a way.*

Remy stood smoothly and stepped forward, toe-to-toe with Dusky. "What did you say?"

She glared back, bristling. "I'm getting her out of the city."

"What the hell for? A fuck? Have you even bedded her, yet? What makes this *gringa*," he sneered the word, "so special that you'd endanger the last of your people?" Remy turned and glared at Sam. He waved a hand at her. "A *puta* is a *puta*. This one's no different than any of the others you've fucked."

Sam shrank under his malicious onslaught, not defending herself. She probably didn't understand Dusky's choice any better than anyone else. *Hell, I don't understand myself.* Dusky's anger built to dangerous levels at Remy's insult. She didn't know what she looked like to the others, but they obviously saw something in her demeanor. Shake shook his head, closed his eyes and rubbed the bridge of his nose while Delva stared. Dusky spun her uncle around to face her. She placed a hand on his chest, pushing as she spoke, walking him backward until his back met the wall. "This is not for a fuck. And what I find special about her is none of your concern. *Mi preciada* is not a whore and I will never allow you to say it again. Is. That. Understood?" She punctuated her last three words by poking his chest with a finger.

Remy looked down at the finger on his chest before glaring back. When he spoke, his words were soft. "You forget who you're talking to, *niña*?"

"No, *tio*. You forget. You are the elder here, not the leader. You advise. I decide. If anyone doesn't like it, there's the door." They stood still for an interminable time, matching each other glare for glare, the other occupants forgotten. Minutes ticked slowly past, the tension palpable and alive, the contest of wills rampaging through their minds and hearts. Remy searched her face, for what she didn't know. Could he see her determination, the undertone of something flowing between she and Sam? Maybe that was why he stared when they were together. Perhaps he felt the strange electrical current that crackled between the women whenever they neared one another. There was danger, yes, and a sense of an impending…something. Could Remy sense that too—the excitement, trepidation, dread and relief all vying for their places in Dusky's heart?

That heart softened as Remy conceded, dropping his gaze. It was victory, but it saddened her. Up until now she'd always taken his counsel, followed his wisdom. This was the first time she'd disagreed with him so thoroughly that they'd banged heads beyond the usual adolescent hurdles. There was no going back, no fallback position that would allow her to say, "It's not my fault, I'm just a child." *I do lead.* She gripped the back of his neck, placing her forehead against his and peering into his eyes. With a final squeeze, she released him and stepped away, scanning Delva and Shake for any indication of rebellion. Shake blew out a breath of relief. Delva simply nodded in recognition and respect. There was no menace. "All right, here's what we need."

* * *

Conway glared at the sergeant standing at attention in front of her desk. He was discovering what many soldiers before him had realized over the course of Conway's career. The frumpy, overweight exterior hid a mind and heart of steel. She'd been stationed in Boise for only two weeks, transferred specifically for this operation, so word hadn't gotten around to the non-com. It showed. While she glared, he stared over her head, eyes cold and face arrogant. "Let me get this right. You didn't put a guard on her door or lock her in the room."

"No, ma'am. You said to be discreet and not draw attention."

"You didn't have her followed when she left base."

"No, ma'am. She wore a tracking device."

Conway picked up the olive drab jumpsuit that had been delivered to the main gate. She pulled at one of the buttons, revealing an electronic device. "And you in your infinite wisdom thought the bug would be all that was necessary?"

The sergeant's scowl deepened and he fairly growled his answer, his tone indicating what he thought of the idiot brass making unreasonable demands. "Yes, ma'am. I wanted to use it as a training exercise for my men. They don't have many opportunities to work with seeker tech."

"A training exercise." She sat back with a sigh, crossing her arms in front of her bountiful chest. "And now we have a woman loose in the city who could conceivably destroy everything we've fought for." She studied him. "What were your specific orders regarding this woman?"

"Maintain surveillance, wait for her to leave post and terminate her."

"Well, one out of three ain't bad, is it, sergeant?" Conway considered her alternatives. She already had the post up in arms hunting for Sam Elias, erstwhile courier and Public Enemy Number One. The next option would be to order soldiers out into the city to locate her. She knew what to do with the blundering sergeant. "You're relieved of duty." She ignored his break from attention to stare at her. "Demoted to private and...oh, I don't know." She studied his paling features idly. "I think a transfer to Death Valley is in order."

"But...you can't do that!" he sputtered.

"That's where you're wrong, private." She stood, leaning her hands on her desk and jutting her chin forward. "Now get the fuck out of my office." The former sergeant stiffened as if to give argument, but something in her steely gaze stopped him. His bluster faded into uncertain fear, and he swallowed. Returning to attention, he snapped a salute and marched out of her office.

Conway sat down, shoving the jumpsuit aside to access her keypad. As she entered the private's new orders, her mind worried the problem of locating her prey. *At least she can't leave the city.* If things turned out well, Sam Elias would come waltzing through the front gates in a few hours. An accident could be arranged at a later date. "Damn it. I wanted this over with by now."

CHAPTER SEVENTEEN

Dusky closed and locked the door on her family. Remy was off to find another set of wheels for Shake. It would be best if he had his own bike should something serious go down. Shake had taken Dusky's motorcycle to circle the wall in search of weakness. He'd stake out the bar afterward as an early warning device should Uncle Sam come knocking. Delva had been dispatched to his contacts in the city in search of a computer with the proper specifications for Sam to download the file. The less Dusky used him, the better. No need to mess up his service time with charges of treason. The Ba'Cho needed all their people to return from the various service branches and become strong again, not have them rotting in military prisons.

She turned away from the door. It was full dark, the three-quarter moon providing the only illumination. Drawn to the window, she stared out, unseeing, ignoring the woman still seated on her bed. Several minutes passed before she felt a hand on her shoulder.

"Why are you doing this?"

Many answers came to Dusky's mind—some acidic, some flippant. Instead, she spoke the truth. "I don't know. It's just something that I have to do." She glanced at Sam, feeling a smile cross her lips. "Why did you come find me?"

A grin played across Sam's face, enhancing her dimples. "I don't know. It was just something I had to do." She wrapped her arms about Dusky's waist.

Dusky luxuriated in the familiarity. She'd been right earlier in the bar. Just before she'd kissed Sam she'd considered backing off. It wouldn't take much to scare Sam away. But Dusky knew that it was already too late. *Hell, it was too late when I first laid eyes on her.* Tantalized by the intoxicating taste of her, Dusky was hooked and nothing else would do. An indescribable undercurrent flowed between them, and though it scared Dusky to her toes, she couldn't push it away. She admitted to herself that she felt apprehensive with the foreign emotions roiling around inside. That didn't matter. Now that she'd plugged in, she couldn't disconnect. *Too late.* She rubbed Sam's back and shoulders, hearing the silky dress whisper as it shifted under her touch. She longed to feel the shiny texture as it slid against Sam's body, wanted to peel it slowly away from her light skin. She closed her eyes, smelling roses. *No more thought.* She slid her hand up into short blond hair, tilting Sam's head back. Once again she tasted the elixir that had claimed her in the bar downstairs, the kiss rapidly changing from gentle to voracious as she claimed what was hers.

Sam stirred beneath her touch, shivering as she clutched at Dusky's shoulders. Dusky's hands enjoyed the delicious sensation of the material as they ran past the small of Sam's back and over the gentle swell of her buttocks. Her fingers dug into the soft flesh, pulling Sam close. Sam's moan pushed Dusky's passion past the flashpoint as she felt the heat settle within her abdomen. Muscles flexed beneath her touch as Sam pressed her hips forward. The sounds Sam made incited her, inflamed her. She had to hear more. She focused her attention on the long, graceful neck, biting and licking and nipping. Soft pleasurable sounds tickled her ears, rewarding her. Dusky took a step forward, pinning Sam against the floor-to-ceiling window. With her quarry pinned, Dusky made good use of both hands, letting them roam up and down the lithe frame at will, caressing, kneading, pinching. Sam gasped at the onslaught, turning her head to the side to expose the fragile skin of her throat. Dusky descended upon it, biting with a growl. She fumbled at the catch of Sam's golden belt, dropping it to the floor with a metallic-sounding *clink*.

Sam's hands no longer gripped Dusky's back. They came around, pushing her away as she squirmed. Her attempt to break free increased Dusky's excitement. She bit down harder on Sam's throat, hands rising to grasp Sam's wrists. Bringing Sam's arms above her head, Dusky held them with one hand, using the other to stroke Sam's breast. The nipple, already swollen with desire, stiffened. Sam's struggles didn't cease, and Dusky pulled back, her hips pinning Sam's to the window. A sense of disappointment washed through her as she studied Sam. Occasionally playing rough was part of the package. If Sam couldn't handle it, no amount of chemistry between them would overcome the discomfort. "What's the matter, *preciada*? Too rough for you?"

"Mmmm…No." Sam gasped, trembling. She turned her head away, glancing outside through the corner of her eye. "The window," she husked. "The people…"

Dusky looked at the window and down to the crowd awaiting admittance. She nodded in comprehension, her burgeoning frustration easing. She released Sam's breast, enjoying the whimper of loss. Dusky rapped her knuckle on the window. "Plastisteel. It's not going to break." She slid her hand behind Sam, pulling forward just enough to allow herself the opportunity to open the zipper of that slinky black dress. Whispering into Sam's ear, she licked a tantalizing earlobe. "As for the people, who cares? They'll see a beautiful woman," soft kiss, "in ecstasy," nibble, "being ravished," lick, "and they'll be jealous." She slid inside the dress, running her fingers across the warmth of Sam's back. "Because they'll never have you." Her fingers tickled Sam's spine, moving inexorably down. Dusky groaned when she realized that Sam hadn't worn underwear. "You're mine, *preciada*."

"Yours." Sam resumed her struggles with a different purpose. She rubbed against Dusky, trying to bring her arms down from their warm prison. She accepted a rough kiss, broke it off, making a fervent effort to partake of Dusky's neck. Dusky denied her, pulling just enough out of reach, and Sam whimpered. Taking another step back, Dusky released Sam altogether. It took a sultry moment before Sam realized she was free. When she did, she closed the distance between them. Dusky fended her off, grabbing her wrists and forcing them down to Sam's side. "Stay."

Sam swallowed and licked her lips, struggling against her need.

Dusky smiled. She released Sam's wrists, taking another step backward, ignoring Sam's sigh of dissatisfaction. She drew the straps of that shiny black dress off Sam's shoulders, revealing creamy skin beneath. The material fluttered to the floor and Sam flushed under Dusky's frank gaze. "You are very beautiful, *preciada*." Sam stood uncertainly in the window, her pulse throbbing visibly at her throat. She was naked to her lover and the world behind her. Dusky watched and waited. Here was Sam's cusp. Would she remain on the edge, grasping for stability and normalcy? Or would she willfully plunge over the edge of her desire, arms open to accept everything that Dusky could give her?

The doubt in Sam's eyes withdrew, replaced with hot determination. She brought her hand up to her breast, a finger softly circling her areola. Dusky stared at the erotic sight, mouth open. Her reaction emboldened Sam, who teased her nipple to full attention. Dusky licked her dry lips, fighting for control as she stripped off her shirt. Sam caressed her abdomen, dropping down to play with damp curls, and Dusky was lost.

* * *

The ringing phone woke him. Blinking wearily, he answered it, looking at the chronometer on his arm. "Shimizu." It wasn't even midnight.

"Harrelson, sir. I think we've figured it out." The younger voice sounded excited.

"Well, spit it out." Shimizu sat up in bed. He was alone.

"The program we acquired—the virus it protects against. Sir, it's a marvelous piece of programming!"

Shimizu sighed in frustration. "Get on with it, Harrelson."

"Yes, sir. The virus appears to be a mutating one, sir. Just when a program has been able to detect and clean it, it'll shift just enough to propagate further. This proggie we've gotten mutates along with the virus, apparently keeping it at bay. We haven't discovered the algorithm it uses to shift, but we're working on it."

"And we don't have the virus?"

"No, sir. Presumably it's with the other courier. The one that we didn't capture."

Irritation flashed through him at the half-assed results of this project. "Report in the morning, Harrelson." He disconnected. After a few minutes thought, he accessed his phone line again, this time dialing out. His entire manner changed from arrogance to submission. "Yes, sir, Shimizu, sir. I realize the hour, sir, but this is very important. Yes, sir. No, sir, but it has to do with Canada GovMin and Uncle Sam. Sir? I would suggest that we hit BoiseGov immediately."

* * *

(Excerpt, Viehl, Anthony. "Japan Rising."
International Computer Engineering Volume 89.
Issue 17 (2057): 56-57)

Next up is Sakimoto Korou, a computer engineer student at the famed Tohoku University in Japan. He has recently won that country's Computer Advancement Science competition with his graduate paper entitled "The Development and Use of Artificial Intelligence in Practical Application." The CAS is one of the premier Japanese competitions with entrants from all over the world vying for acclaim. Winners can expect to receive lucrative research grants and job positions in the corporate world. Sakimoto is considered a shining intellect who will light the way of his country well into the twenty-second century.

Not everyone has good things to say about Sakimoto's breakthrough paper, which discusses the use of artificial intelligence in all aspects of life, including the monitoring of functions in manned orbital space stations. Dr. Joseph Keenan, a spokesperson for the International Consortium of Ethical Science said, "There's a reason AI work has been banned by the United Nations: Who's to say that any AI will fully comprehend the world? Will it understand life and death? And who are we to enslave a life we create, should it actually be possible?"

While Dr. Sakimoto has refused to comment on the ICES' concerns, Shizou Uda, president of Tohoku University and long-time advocate of removing limitations against science, has responded to Dr. Keenan's concerns. "A paper on theoretical applications can hardly be cause for such dismay. Yes, actual programming of artificial intelligence is outlawed, but this isn't programming. This is a paper on application! Dr. Keenan has always been an alarmist."

Regardless of "is he/isn't he," the fact remains that Dr. Sakimoto has been recruited to work for the renowned Saburo Tech. Saburo Tech rose to prominence with its cutting edge SynFl™, an entertainment wetware system that allows the user to experience the recorded senses and emotions of other individuals. Using such capital, Saburo Tech has expanded its holdings into multiple aspects of computer programming with heavy interests in space station technology.

CHAPTER EIGHTEEN

(Excerpt, Wall Street Journal Weekend Special, Sunday, May 13ᵗʰ, 2057)

Three Tech Stocks on the Rise!

Looking for a profitable company in which to invest? Haven't a clue where to start looking? We ran a check on the tech sector for stocks indicating tenaciousness and upward momentum. These stocks are those that have seen consistent increases over the last five years. (We made certain that these companies also had positive earnings during that time.)

Interactive Chart: Press Play to compare changes in analyst ratings over the last two years for the stocks mentioned below. Analyst ratings sourced from Wyatt Research.

Play

And here's a price-weighted index below. We've monitored their performance relative to the S&P 500 index over the last month. To access a complete analysis of this list's recent performance, *click here.*

(List sorted by market cap.)
**LOAD UP THREE CORPORATIONS -
Yamaguchi is one, check the encyclopedia for other tech companies.**
1. DiBilio Coporation (DBC): The world's premier producer of cyberdecks and related equipment. Market cap of $334.90B. The stock is currently trading at 4.67% above its 20-Day SMA, 6.35% above its 50-Day SMA, and 19.21% above its 200-Day SMA. The stock has gained 6.8% over the last year.
2. Saburo Tech (SBT): Operates in the wetware entertainment industry. Market cap of $9.70B. The stock is currently trading at 8.19% above its 20-Day SMA, 3.90% above its 50-Day SMA, and 16.57% above its 200-Day SMA. The stock has gained 53.5% over the last year.
3. Yamaguchi, Inc. (YAMA): Provides integrated computer systems for space habitats, satellites and orbital stations. Market cap of $5.81B. The stock is currently trading at 3.55% above its 20-Day SMA, 4.67% above its 50-Day SMA, and 9.52% above its 200-Day SMA. The stock has gained 21.66% over the last year.
Disclosure: Article author has no position in any stocks mentioned and no plans to initiate any positions within the next three days.

* * *

Conway wearily rubbed her eyes. It wasn't quite dawn. The sky hadn't begun to lighten, but what little nature was still present in the world held its collective breath in anticipation of it. "So you haven't found her, then?"

"No, ma'am. We've located two of the three nomads that brought her in, however." The recently promoted sergeant stood at rigid attention.

Chewing her lower lip, Conway considered her options. *Either the kid knows the jig is up, which is highly unlikely, or she's out having a good time and will be back for business hours.* "Where are the Lichii Ba'Cho?"

"They've set up residence at Ritzy's for the night. We've seen the two men exiting and entering the building. Right now, the younger one is under surveillance in the bar. The older one seems to have a room there."

Conway remembered Sam Elias's adamant defense of the nomads. *Maybe we could killfile two birds with one script.* "Get hold of the local authorities. Let's have the bar raided. Of course, the military will 'help.'" She pulled her keypad to her and began typing. "Let's see if we can arrange an accident for the nomads. I think chances are pretty good that the courier's with them."

"Yes, ma'am!" The sergeant saluted smartly and left the office.

* * *

Sam opened her eyes. She lay on the bed in Dusky's room, a strong body wrapped around her, a sheet draped over the both of them. With a soft smile, she turned her head and studied Dusky as she slept, idly caressing the upper arm that crossed over her, tracing the ritual scarring beneath her fingertips. Outside it was full dark, but it was a darkness of

silent waiting, of the quiet before the storm, where everything
held breathlessly still and awaited the rising sun. The moon
had set long ago, and the only illumination in the room was
light from streetlamps and the Ritzy's sign. She reached up to
brush a lock of dark hair away from Dusky's face, marveling
at the soft unconscious smile her action elicited. *So sweet.*
More words came forth—pure, innocent, loving. Sam's brow
furrowed. *But is this for me? Or am I just the one in her bed?*
What would happen when Dusky awoke? Gently, so as not
to arouse her, Sam eased out of Dusky's arms and off the bed.
She scooped up Dusky's discarded shirt and donned it rather
than her dress, wanting to have Dusky with her despite their
physical separation. She quietly curled up on the floor in the
corner by the window, staring out at the morning.

She knew this wasn't all some romantic lark. Dusky lived
in a completely different culture. In that world, Sam was a
gringa, a foreigner. *Not of the body*, she thought with a smirk,
remembering an ancient science fiction vid. Things were
going to change, as soon as Dusky woke up. This afterglow
of—*Is it love?*—would be confronted by the harsh light of
reality. Sam remembered the previous night's discussion of
Aryans and scalps and wars. *Can I live with that?* Could she
exist knowing that every day would bring a new opportunity
to kill or be killed? Knowing she might have to kill? Or die?
I don't know. Was that option even open considering Remy's
dissatisfaction with her? Dusky stirred, rolling over on her
side. Sam watched her frown in her sleep, hand searching
for her bedmate. She didn't wake, clutching a pillow as a
substitute, subsiding into slumber.

What if this isn't an option? Her gaze roamed the graceful
curves of her lover. She imagined Dusky in Canada, living
with her, meeting her acquaintances, plugging into the local
scene. *No.* Sam shook her head. It would kill Dusky to live
like that, and the Lichii Ba'Cho wouldn't have a leader. Deep
down inside, Sam didn't want to be the one responsible for the
broken woman Dusky would become in that scenario. *Never*

cage the wild. She sighed and stared back out the window. All of it was moot anyway if she couldn't get out of Boise. Azteca wanted her dead, Uncle Sam wanted her dead. What about Canada GovMin? Why send her to certain death unless they were involved too? *And who's involved with who, anyway?* No answers were forthcoming. *Elias, if you get out of this with your skin, you stick to small contracts from now on. No more government involvement, regardless of the money.* It was a long time before she heard a low voice.

"*Preciada?*"

Sam looked back at the bed. Dusky watched her, her cyberoptic eye flashing in the minimal light. Sam smiled and rose to her feet, crossing the small room. The oversized white shirt slid easily from her shoulders and she eased back into the bed.

Dusky covered her with the sheet and wrapped herself around Sam. "Are you okay?" She cradled Sam, brushing her fingers through Sam's hair.

"Yeah. Just thinking."

When she said nothing more, Dusky caressed her cheek and jaw with her thumb. "About...?" she prompted, waiting.

Sam gave a slight shrug and looked away. "A question you asked downstairs last night." Pause. "Now what?" She looked back at Dusky.

Dusky nodded in understanding and laid back, holding Sam close as she stared at the ceiling. "Now, we survive. We take it one day at a time and get through this feedback. There's not much else to do."

Resigned, Sam nodded, not hearing what she hoped to hear. "Could I ask for your help in getting me back to Canada then?" Her question was hopeful. She wanted to spend as much time in Dusky's presence as possible before their inevitable parting. "I may be in danger from Canada GovMin and I have no way to get across the border legally."

Dusky's eyes narrowed. "Do you want to go back to Canada?"

"Well, no." Sam shrugged again, hardly daring to hope.

Dusky rolled over, propping herself up on an elbow, and looked down at Sam. "What do you want, Sam Elias?"

The sound of her name coming for the first time from Dusky's mouth startled her enough that she answered truthfully. "I want to stay with you." She mentally smacked herself in the forehead as soon as the words were out. Angered at her inability to keep her mouth shut, she broke away from Dusky's grasp, sitting up on the edge of the bed and wrapping her arms around herself. *Zero, zero, zero!* The bed shifted beneath her, and body heat radiated against her back. Dusky's arms wrapped around her from behind, breasts pressing into Sam's back.

Warm breath whispered into Sam's left ear. "Then stay with me." Not giving Sam a chance to respond, Dusky continued in a low voice. "I told you, you're mine, *preciada*. That hasn't changed." Sam leaned back into the embrace. "Do you have someone else? Someone at home?"

Sam couldn't find her voice, resorting to a whisper. "No." *Be honest, Elias, if you did, you'd drop whoever it was in a hot minute for this.*

"Then what is it? Why are you fighting this?"

Sam snorted tearfully, entwining her arms with Dusky's. "Why? Your uncle hates me, both Uncle Sam and Azteca are after me, Canada might be after me too. Even if things work out I'll be an illegal alien here. I can't get any work. I'll be a burden." She snorted again. "And if your uncle doesn't hate me enough now, he'll hate me for that." The tears came in earnest, releasing the tension and stress she'd suffered the last two days. Dusky held her, supported her, humming a quiet song as tears of anger, fear and frustration fell. Eventually the sobs faded, the tears slowed and Sam sniffled.

Dusky used a corner of the sheet to dry Sam's face. "Feel better?"

She gave Dusky a watery smile. "Yeah. Some."

"Good." Dusky pulled away to lay on the bed, propped up against the wall. She beckoned Sam to her and they snuggled together. "First, Remy doesn't hate you. He's an old man, set in his ways. He's just seen nearly his entire family wiped out by racist *gringos*." Long fingers caressed Sam's arm and shoulder. "He worries about me. He wants me to find a husband and give him lots of little ones to dote on in his old age." She closed her eyes a moment, and Sam wondered what she was thinking. Before she could ask, Dusky opened them and continued. "Second, this mess will work out. Hell, the government's been after us for one thing or another for forty years. It's slow and clunky and it'll take forever for it to catch us. The corps just want what's in your head, and we're gonna give it to them." She gave Sam a squeeze. "And Canada... Who cares? They sent you to die," she growled. "It's easy to get forged citizenship papers. We've got connections in several cities." She hugged Sam close, whispering, "Besides, I want you to stay too."

Heart beating hard in her chest, Sam dared to ask. "You do?"

"Yes. You're *mi preciada*. I don't know how or why, but I feel that we belong together." Dusky swallowed, her eyes darting around in an uncharacteristic expression of nervousness. "Sam Elias, I am Dusky Holt, leader of the Lichii Ba'Cho, and I love you."

Sam stopped breathing, staring at her. *She loves me?* Her mind chortled. *Me?* She wrapped her mind around that thought, not realizing what the silence was doing to Dusky. When Sam didn't respond, Dusky's face became stone, and she relaxed her grip. As the arms loosened their hold, Sam's heart fluttered, slightly panicked. She clutched Dusky to her, not relinquishing her grasp. "I love you too." The rigid mask broke apart under Sam's gaze and fell away, revealing a beautiful young woman. Sam smiled.

"You do?" Dusky whispered. She suddenly looked like a four-year-old at Christmas. "Then you'll stay?" Panic chased away the childlike doubt. "No! You don't have to answer yet. Let's get through this feedback first." She gathered Sam up in her arms.

There was an insistent rap on the door, and Shake's voice came through. "Dusky?"

Dusky grumbled, disentangling herself. "That boy has some serious work to do on his timing." She flashed a smile at Sam's giggle. Climbing out of bed, she threw on her shirt and padded to the door. Sam wrapped the sheet around herself, watching Dusky's hips sway and the muscles in her legs flex. *Beautiful doesn't cut it at all.*

Shake fairly burst into the room when the door opened. He grinned apologetically at the half-naked women. "We got trouble downstairs. Army's chippin' in—weapons and all."

CHAPTER NINETEEN

Dusky sent Shake to gather his things and roust Remy. Within minutes she was dressed in her riding leathers, strapping boots onto her feet. She'd thrown clothing at Sam—the shirt she had worn earlier and a pair of soft trousers. "Roll up the leggings. That'll have to do until we get out of here." She checked her weapons with care. Their grenade launcher was gone, but she still had the sniper rifle on her bike in the basement garage, three knives, a .45 automatic and an Armalite 44 heavy auto pistol. She also had three fragmentation grenades that she transferred to the pockets of her leather jacket. After a moment's thought, she handed the .45 to Sam, ignoring her nervous gulp. Sam took the handgun, blinking at the heavy weight in her palm. "There's the safety, here are some extra clips." Dusky took the gun back and pulled back the chamber, expertly catching the round that popped out of it. "Release, drop the clip, insert the new one, lock and load. Got it?"

"Got it." Sam showed her comprehension by repeating the procedure. She fumbled but had a certain level of native efficiency Dusky was pleased to see. A pounding at the door interrupted the lesson. Someone shouted in alarm down the hall, a yell that escalated into a scream as a rattle of gunfire went off. It stopped, and the door shuddered under another onslaught.

"Dammit! Shake was followed." Dusky shoved Sam to one side, away from the door. "Get down!" She held her Armalite loosely in her left hand, staring intently at the door with Sam crouched behind her.

There was more shooting. The wood around the lock disintegrated. Light glared through the holes, illuminating the smoke and dust of the destruction. Dusky lifted the Armalite, taking careful aim. The door slammed open, and something metallic rolled across the floor. *Fuck! Grenade!* Dusky moved without thought, the deadly dance begun. She fired two shots at the door to discourage further invasion as she dived through the air. Landing beside the still rolling grenade, she used a well-aimed kick and sent it flying back out into the corridor. She had barely enough time to return to Sam's side, driving the two of them to the ground before the explosion jolted the room. More screams gurgled off into moans. As the dust settled, Dusky picked herself up and edged forward. She darted past the doorframe, getting a quick glance of the hall. Nothing moved. Sam shifted, and Dusky held up a hand, indicating stillness. Sam nodded, staying put. Dusky dropped to the floor, easing her head around the jamb for a better look. Three soldiers lay in the destruction of their grenade. Two were in pieces, but one had been a few meters down the hall. She was still alive, moaning and writhing as she gathered her guts in restless hands. At the far end were the bodies of two civilians. *The screamers.* There were no signs of Dusky's pack mates, yet. She felt relief that Shake had gotten out of the area before the military's arrival. She pushed to her feet and rushed out to kneel beside the third soldier, continuing to scan the hall for enemies. "Looking for me?"

"Ba'Cho...?" The soldier moaned, coughing weakly, blood spattering out of her mouth. She shook her head no. "Elias. Courier."

Dusky's face grew grim. "Wrong answer." She pumped a round into the woman's head. A faint sound behind her made her spin, and she saw Sam duck back inside the room. Dusky looked down at the dead woman at her knees, trying to dredge up a sense of guilt for her actions. Normal people seemed to think that killing scarred you forever, and maybe it did. If so, Dusky had been scarred for so long, it no longer affected her. *But it affects Sam.* Here was another hurdle for them to overcome. They could talk all they wanted about Sam joining the Ba'Cho, but would she be able to handle the violent reality of her new life?

A room door eased open a crack, and she automatically sighted the single eye peering out at her. The person gave a shriek and slammed the door closed, a series of noises indicating the locks engaging. "Time's a'wasting." Dusky returned to the room to find Sam sitting against the wall, eyes closed, gasping for breath. She knelt beside her. "Put your head between your knees. Breathe deeply, slow count of five." Sam complied. Her breathing evened out and, after a few moments, she raised her head. Dusky caressed her hair. "You okay to move now?"

"Yeah." Sam gave a wan smile and hefted the .45 with bravado.

Pleased, Dusky nodded and planted a kiss on her forehead. "We've got to get to Remy and Shake." She stood, helping Sam to her feet and breaking away to grab her saddlebag. "I need you to follow my orders implicitly." Turning back, she stared intently at Sam until she received an answering nod. "Okay. Stay behind me, keep your eyes open." She moved to the door. "Let's go."

They moved through the halls. Noises filtered up from the bar below—gunshots, screams, explosions. The fire alarm blared, set off by smoke from weapons, adding to the cacophony of sound and confusion. Dusky heard more shots on their floor, but she didn't yet see the threat. Not all the overnight guests were content to cower in their rooms, small wonder considering at least half probably thought this raid was aimed at them. The brave ones dashed about the halls in various stages of undress, fleeing, grabbing gear and looking for exits. The chaos worked fine for Dusky as it camouflaged her activities. Dusky and Sam rounded a corner, finding much the same scene they had left in their hallway. Two soldiers were down and a third was prone, using a dead comrade as cover while he traded shots with Remy and Shake.

Dusky shoved Sam back, took aim and killed the attacker. "Uncle, it's clear." Seconds later, Remy and Shake trotted toward her, weapons and gear in hands. "Everybody okay?" She scanned them both, relieved that they appeared uninjured. Raising an eyebrow at Shake, she grinned. "You were followed, little man. Don't let it happen again." She cuffed him on his good arm and turned away, ignoring his blush of embarrassment. She led them toward the emergency stairs, the destination of everyone else on this floor. "You remember how many there were, Shake?"

"A dozen, up to twenty. They're working with the bacon on this raid. Lots of blacksuits down there too."

Sam frowned. "Blacksuits?"

Remy brought up the rear. "Police. Riot gear."

"Oh." She shook her head. "I'm going to need a slang dictionary for this place."

They found a fire exit door, not because of the flickering "Exit" sign above it, but because of the mass of humanity huddled around it. The door was closed and no one seemed to be in a hurry to leave. "Get the fuck out of the way." Dusky shoved people aside. One burly man took umbrage at her brisk manner, and she pistol-whipped him as she passed, knocking him on his butt. When he prepared to stand, blood trickling from his mouth, he found himself looking at the business end of a .45 automatic.

"Don't." Sam's voice was firm, backed up by Remy and Shake bristling with armament.

The man raised his hands in surrender, a silly grin coming to his bloody lips. "Okay. I won't. It's chill, input."

Dusky made it to the door. A dead woman and two wounded men had been dragged to the sides. A third man applied pressure to a wound; the copious bleeding seemed a good indication there'd be two dead soon. She knelt beside him. "What's going on?"

"Troops on the stairs. Firing at everything that moves." His patient went into convulsions, dying in a sudden smelly moment as all the muscles in his body relaxed, flooding the area with urine, feces and blood. "Dammit!"

Dusky growled in exasperation. She stood and turned to the crowd behind her. "Anybody have any weapons?" Several did, but all were either knives or small caliber pistols. She shook her head. "Stupid sheep." Raising her voice, she asked, "Have you tried the other stairs?"

A woman in back answered. "Yeah, same thing there."

"Remy? Shake? You got anything?"

Both men shook their heads no, and Remy spoke. "No, Dusk. You still have grenades?"

"Yeah." She pursed her lips as she considered her options. *Three grenades. Three sets of stairs.* She eyed the crowd, who looked to her for direction. Most of them were small-time hoods, more than willing to bow down to a trio of nomads packing extensive armament. Picking two men, she pulled two grenades out of her pocket, handing one to each. "Go to the other stairs. When you hear mine go off, toss these down. Then rush the fuckers." She watched them nod and trot away. A handful went after them, but the majority remained with her. She figured there were equal numbers at each of the exits and wasn't worried about lack of manpower. "C'mon, let's get these bodies out of the way."

A few minutes later, the corpses were stacked down the hall, the wounded man with them. The Ba'cho huddled by the door, checking their ammunition and preparing for the run. All the civilians had backed away. Dusky glanced at them with disdain. *Nothing but cattle.* She watched Sam check her weapon for the third time, hands shaking as she mouthed the order of operation Dusky had taught her.

Remy followed Dusky's gaze. He studied Sam. "You okay?"

Startled, Sam blinked. "Um…yeah, I guess." She shrugged. "This is all kinda, you know…new."

He nodded solemnly. "You'll get used to it. Adapt. It's not always this way." He took a deep breath. "I apologize for my earlier behavior and words."

Sam stared for a silent moment. "Accepted."

Remy nodded.

Dusky grinned, her heart filling with pride at her uncle's attempt at burying the hatchet. "All right. Let's do it."

* * *

Amelia Lukich, newly appointed sergeant in charge of this mission, stood at the base of a fire exit with a private. Blood dripped down from above onto her crisp uniform, but she didn't mind. It just meant she was doing her job well. The platoon had lost contact with first squad. First had been sent up when the nomad boy had run from the bar. Second was deployed on the streets outside the exits, picking off the few that managed to escape the bar. She was with third squad on the stairs, keeping the hotel patrons pinned above. As soon as the police finished in the bar, she'd have second squad move up to her position and she'd help take the upper levels. No way in hell was she was going to end up like her previous sergeant, demoted and sent to Bumfuck, America. She wanted Lt. Colonel Conway to be very happy with her.

Someone pushed one of the metal fire doors open above her. It made a distinctive sound, and the private on point eased up the stairs, peering through his rifle sights. She brought her rifle up to her shoulder and followed. A metallic clatter gave her pause. *What the hell?* Lukich froze as she saw the round object bounce past her down the stairs. "Grenade!" She surged up the stairs, shoving the private forward.

The explosion picked her up like so much trash and tossed her forward. She felt the white-hot pain of shrapnel shredding her back and legs. Falling forward, she pinned the private's legs. Above them, the door burst open and the nomads she hunted were suddenly there. An elderly man with the braided beard raised his pistol. There was a flash from the muzzle and then it was dark.

* * *

Remy finished off the soldiers in the stairwell, and two more explosions blew in the distance indicating the other grenades had gone off. Dusky snorted. "At least they can follow direction."

Shake pushed past Remy to take point, probably wanting to redeem himself for leading the soldiers right to them. He fired another shot into the private as he passed, shoving the corpses aside with his foot. Sam ground her teeth, fighting against her queasy stomach as she looked everywhere but at the remains of a man and a woman who had once had families, ambitions and lives. She focused on Shake's back, ignoring the dead soldiers.

At the bottom of the stairs was the door leading out onto the third-floor balcony of the bar. It teetered on one hinge, the metal dented and torn where the grenade had hit it at close range, but was still in place. Shake slipped past and eased toward the next landing. Sneaking a peek down, he moved slowly forward, stepping carefully on the metal stairs. Behind him, Remy followed, and Dusky brought up the rear. Sam glanced back to catch Dusky glaring at the civilians hovering in the doorway upstairs, her threat imminent. None of them appeared ready to thwart her silent order, and Sam felt a panicked burble of humor. Dusky paused as she passed the bodies, holstering her pistol and picking up one of the rifles.

Sam swallowed hard, not wanting the reminder. She slipped past the broken door and followed Remy. On the next landing, something warm dripped on her arm. She glanced over sharply as another drop of blood splattered on her from above. She grimaced in disgust, wanting to rage at the injustice of the killing and destruction. She also wanted to wipe the blood off her arm, knowing it would only smear and stain her soul. There was another part of her, one primal and feral, a part that had long lay dormant beneath the facade of civilization. That part wanted to survive. At all costs. She inhaled deeply, counting to five, and exhaled the same way, regulating her breathing as Dusky had instructed. Continuing down the stairs, she ignored the blood on her arm. *Deal, Elias.* Remy must have sensed something. He glanced back at her as he passed the door to Ritzy's second balcony, a speculative look on his face. Sam didn't know what he saw, but he nodded in satisfaction and continued on.

Shake reached the first-floor landing, signaling that it was clear. This door opened out onto the main bar. A hell of a firefight was happening inside, the stairwell ringing with the sound of it. Apparently, some patrons didn't particularly care for the police and were making their opinions known. The door was dented in places, though Sam didn't know whether the damage was from their current situation or previous raids. Shake scanned it with a practiced eye, pointing at a pair of wires. "Alarmed."

Dusky moved past, bringing Sam up between the two men. "Let's see if we can make it to the garage." Remy took the rear guard as Dusky pulled point.

They met no resistance as they reached the bottom of the stairwell and the final door. There was a frantic moment as an alarm blared, scaring Sam so bad she almost fired her pistol into the wall. The civilians from their floor had finally made it to the first floor and had opened the door there. The sound from the firefight roared painfully in the echoing confines, sounding as if all the minions of hell were at war. Acrid smells of plastique, cordite and gunpowder drifted over them.

Dusky had to yell to be heard. "Well, so much for a silent attack." Ignoring the similar wiring on the door before her, she pushed it open and dived into the basement garage, rolling and rifle ready. If the alarm added its voice to the din, Sam couldn't tell. Her heart beat a counterpoint staccato in her chest, all her attention on Dusky's absence. *It's so loud! Will I even hear if she gets shot?* Shake dashed after Dusky. Remy put a hand on Sam's shoulder, keeping her pinned to the wall inside the stairwell.

Nothing happened.

Remy peeked around the corner. Gauging the situation safe, he ushered Sam out into the garage, pushing her down beside an ancient recreational vehicle. Shake had taken refuge behind a beat-up hovercar, and Dusky peered over a modern electric model to scan the parking area. The garage wasn't completely abandoned. A few people from the other fire exits had made it down, more interested in getting away from the raid than dealing with flak from heavily armed nomads. It was quieter here, especially after the door closed behind them, muffling the alarms and blasts from upstairs.

Deeming it safe, Dusky rose to her feet. "Let's get to the bikes." She led the way as they trotted across the cement.

There were a number of parked motorcycles. Remy pulled up short, reaching out to grab Sam before she got too close to Dusky's bike. Puzzled, she watched as the others held back too. *What?* Remy glanced over the vehicles with a practiced eye, circling each one, squatting to stare at the engines. He carefully examined a rifle attached to his bike, making some adjustment to it before slamming it back into its scabbard. On each bike he fiddled with something. *Is he clearing booby traps?* When satisfied, he nodded. Dusky and Shake surged forward to mount their bikes. Shake's new ride was as battered as his last one had been. Dusky shoved the scavenged rifle into her empty scabbard and attached her saddlebags. Straddling the bike, she kick-started the engine. She held out her hand to help Sam climb aboard.

Remy took the lead, Shake taking the rear guard. They edged forward at a glacial pace, weaving between refugees fleeing the firefight as they made their way to the exit. One idiot made a grab at Dusky as they passed, presumably to hijack the motorcycle. Sam shuddered and buried her face in Dusky's shoulders, the spray of arterial blood from the man's throat catching her on the right. Dusky's knife disappeared and she squeezed Sam's hand at her waist before returning her attention to driving. Sam cursed all the violent American videos she'd watched as a rebellious youngster. They hadn't done anything to prepare her for this savage reality.

A Chevy squealed as it fishtailed by, narrowly missing Remy. It hit a man on foot ahead of them, tossing him to one side to smash against a pillar. The Chevy didn't stop, speeding through the entrance and to freedom. The driver's liberty didn't last long. A hollow metal *phumph* echoed in the street, and Sam peered over Dusky's shoulder to see what caused it. The Chevy exploded in a gigantic fireball of orange and yellows, making Sam gasp. Momentum kept it going forward on fiery rubber tires, wobbling as it struggled to a stop, lighting up the street.

"Shit!" Dusky pulled to one side of the garage entrance. The heat of the fire blazed strong enough for Sam to feel it against her face despite the distance. Remy and Shake joined them. "Stay here." Dusky dismounted, leaving Sam to guard the bikes, her pack mates following her.

Another car raced through the garage entrance, making a hard right turn. This time, Sam saw the brilliant flash of an anti-tank missile from across the street. Whoever was manning the missile launcher was a crack shot. The car exploded. *Is that even possible?* Sam had always thought those weapons were slow and clunky when it came to aiming. She overheard Dusky answering her question before she could ask it.

"Must be using heat seekers."

"Maybe we won't put out enough heat," Shake suggested.

Remy nixed that hope. "No. Heat seekers are pretty sensitive. They've probably calibrated them just for motorcycles. Anything with a larger heat source would just be easier to hit."

Dusky glared in fury. "Well, hell! Now what?"

While they pondered their rapidly dwindling options, Sam watched as a few civilians ran out of the garage. *Maybe it will be easier to get away on foot.* Before she could fully grasp the promising notion, she heard automatic gunfire from across the street. No pedestrians survived.

"Shit!" Dusky cursed again.

Sam felt despair. All these people were innocent victims, collateral damage, only guilty of having chosen to come to Ritzy's. *It's my fault.* She stared at Dusky, recognizing the expression of defeat forming on her beautiful face. Sam couldn't bear the thought of that face becoming still, that body she had come to know so intimately bursting from bullets, the blood cooling on the concrete as the blood on Sam's arm had already cooled. *I can stop this.* She brought her leg over, climbing off Dusky's motorcycle. If she left the garage, went out onto the street, the soldiers would get what they had come for and leave everyone else alone.

Dusky glanced back at her movement. "Don't even think about it," she snarled. She left her view of the street, blocking Sam's path and holding her shoulders. "It won't change a damned thing."

"It will, Dusky. If I give them what they want, they'll be done. They'll stop."

"What about what I want?"

Sam sniffled, reaching up to cup Dusky's cheek.

Remy appeared beside them. "That's a crock, *gringa*. It is what it is. You go out there now, they'll get what they came for, and then they'll sweep the rest of us into a hole and bury us."

"Yeah, *querida*." Shake had joined them. "It's too late now."

A wave of sorrow swept over Sam. Before she could speak, heavy weapons began firing out on the street. They all turned to see a riot car had sped around the corner, blocking the tank's view of the garage entrance. Weapons on the far side had targeted Uncle Sam's forces, forestalling another heat seeker launch. The driver's window opened and a familiar face looked out at them.

"C'mon! Let's go!" Delva yelled.

Needing no more encouragement, the Lichii Ba'Cho scrambled onto their bikes. They peeled out of the garage and down the street. In seconds, the riot car followed. It pulled up close to Dusky, who had taken the lead.

"Follow me. I've got a safe flop." Delva pulled forward at Dusky's nod.

Sam clutched her lover, her face buried against Dusky's back, mourning the loss of life she'd witnessed and disgusted with her sense of glee at escaping death yet again. *I'm a coward. A coward and a zero.*

CHAPTER TWENTY

Whoever had designed the battle room had seen too many science fiction videos. It was large and cavernous with the majority of the light emitting from huge computer monitors along one wall. Several workstations sat in rows facing the display boards, each with its own individual lights, manned by people plugged into the net. Others bustled back and forth with files and paperwork on an overhead catwalk. Shimizu sat with three other people in the command center, a large half circle of complicated machinery. He was there as an observer for his employer, nothing more. Still, the carefully constructed atmosphere did highlight the underlying tension and excitement of this exercise. The largest display on the wall was a simple line drawing of the world map. Several smaller displays showed current rates of money and stock exchanges. Two, however, held maps of Boise and the surrounding area. Four groupings of red triangles and blue dots, two of each, glowed stark against the darkness. The triangles were several miles away from the white line of Boise's wall, and the dots quite a bit closer.

The man seated beside Shimizu wore a jumpsuit that strained against its fastenings. This was his domain despite the fact that they were on the same management track. "All right, people, let's look good." He leaned over his console and spoke into a microphone. "Report!"

One set of triangles blinked. "Beta One in position." The other set blinked. "Beta Two in position." Then each set of blue dots flashed to indicate open mics as they responded. "Comrade One in position. Comrade Two in position."

"Let's do it, then. Commence radio jamming." The man leaned back in his chair, a frown on his face. "Beta One and Two, fire at will. Repeat. Fire at will."

Shimizu leaned forward to watch the screens, daydreaming. Had he made different decisions earlier in his career, he'd be running this show instead of the fat tub beside him. *Security's not that different from military.* The triangles didn't move, but their radio chatter was broadcast in the room as he toyed with the idea of taking a lateral promotion into the Military Development Department.

* * *

Conway sat at her desk, chewing a cuticle. The raid had been engaged at Ritzy's for a quarter hour. The last communication with Lukich had told her that the squad sent into the upper floors had lost radio contact with the rest of the platoon. According to what she'd picked up from the police scanner on her desk, a booster gang had been in residence in the bar when the raid had commenced. The platoon of blacksuits had been severely hobbled, pinned by their fire, and the police had been forced to send in their SWAT team. The fighting was ferocious with casualties on both sides. The loss of multiple law enforcement officers was dreadful, but the cause sound. *Maybe I should send another platoon.* She mentally shook her head. The fewer people who knew about the operation, the better. She leaned back in her chair and ran fingers through her short, graying hair. Listening to the radio chatter, she scowled impatiently. *This wait is going to kill me.*

So involved was she with the police scanner that she didn't realize that a distant air raid siren had started yowling over the city. As the sound registered, she heard a closer one take up the mournful call. *What the hell?* Her building shook, followed by a second more intense rocking. This time, the accompanying explosion reached her ears, as well. She jumped to her feet, threw open the door and looked into a chaos-filled hallway. Grabbing a passing soldier, she demanded, "What the hell is going on out there?"

The soldier, a young man barely out of his teens, stared at her. "We're under attack, ma'am," he squeaked, freckles standing out against a pale face.

"I figured that! By who?"

"A corporation, ma'am! Azteca, I think."

Conway left the soldier, dashing back into her office. She picked up the phone and tried to get hold of headquarters, receiving a busy signal. "Damn it!" She smashed the phone down. "Now is not the time for this shit!" If they were lucky, Mountain Home Air Force Base had been alerted and backup was on the way. If they weren't, Boise was screwed.

I have to make sure Elias is dusted. With communications in an uproar from an attack, her only option was to go to Ritzy's and see the job done herself. Mind made up, she opened a desk drawer and pulled out an Ares Light Fire pistol. Checking the load and scooping up extra clips of ammunition, she headed for the door. *Next stop, motor pool.*

Miles away from the base, the Azteca Corporation tactical group nicknamed Beta One launched another fiery gift to Boise from its perch on Table Rock. It was lovingly wrapped in the white and orange plastic of a missile. Within seconds, it soared past the Boise Wall and began a graceful arc downward. Conway stepped out of the building. Hearing a whistling noise, she looked up. In eerie slow motion, she saw the cone of a missile head falling from the sky. There was no time to dodge or run, she could only watch as it approached with lethal speed. As it impacted with her frumpy body, it exploded, taking out her office and a good portion of the building in which it had been housed.

Justice had been served.

* * *

Positioned along a ridge south of Interstate 84, Azteca Assault Force Comrade Two sat just within firing range of the Boise Wall. Their commander waited until the attack from Betas One and Two were well underway before ordering his men into the fray. "Fire!" Two Panther cannons sent their payloads to the South Gate in a flare of phosphorous. In the darkness, the projectiles lanced through the sky, barely visible until they reached the twin spires of the gate towers. Two glorious fireballs rose high into the night sky, raining shrapnel and body parts down upon the unsuspecting garrison below. The commander grinned as he watched the mass panic at the base of the burning towers through his binocs. The troops regrouped and hardened their position at the permanent machine gun berms and concrete foxholes. "Again!" Another volley of cannon fire hit the wall, one compounding the damage on the left tower, but the other falling too short of its target. He swore but didn't take his cannoneer to task— Panthers had their uses, but they also had a tendency to lose their targeting capability at the recoil. Instead, he watched the scramble at the gate. "Fire at will."

Though Comrade Two pounded at the gate, their attack seemed ineffectual. Uncle Sam's troops pinpointed their location and fired back, driving Comrade Two under cover. The Azteca unit continued to attack, getting nowhere as the army harassed them. Eventually reinforcements arrived from their base, some relieving the fighters in their berms and others attempting to put out the fires that the cannons had started. The walls around the gate were pitted with damage, but no worse for wear. Grinning, the commander flicked his wrist to access his radio link. "Commence radio jamming."

"Yes, sir!"

"Comrade Two to Comrade One. We are engaged, repeat, we are engaged. She's all yours."

There was a tinny response in his ear. "Comrade One to Comrade Two. Thanks, partner! Give 'em hell! Out."

From the darkness of the north foothills three large riot cars and multiple smaller support vehicles roared toward the Foothills Gate. Filled with shock troopers, they zipped past an ancient pioneer cemetery to their right. As they neared the Boise Wall, they spread out and opened fire, surprising the soldiers who moments earlier had been disappointed that all the action was taking place across town.

Time to take the city.

CHAPTER TWENTY-ONE

No one appeared to follow the Lichii Ba'Cho. Uncle Sam seemed preoccupied with extricating what was left of its people from the fiasco at Ritzy's. The nomads had a few moments' grace as they roared away from the mayhem on Warm Springs. Sam held tight to Dusky's waist, face still buried between her shoulder blades. Dusky peered over her shoulder. "You okay back there?" Sam squeezed her and she felt a slight nod. Dusky scowled. The way her *preciada* clung to her, she doubted Sam was okay at all. If she'd been hurt, Shake would have seen it and said something by now. *It has to wait until we get where we're going.*

Air raid sirens crawled up from the depths, shouting across the city. Dusky kept her eyes moving, seeking danger. She wondered if the sirens were a way to warn the city of their passage through the streets, but that was overkill even for the government. Though the rumble and vibration of her bike drowned out most sound and sensation, she saw what looked like a missile streaking by overhead. Something huge was going down in Boise; it was more than just the raid on Ritzy's. There wasn't time for discussion or speculation until Delva could get them to safety.

They cruised along North Third, within sight of the Boise Wall. On Fort Street, they took a left, following that with another left onto Franklin, abandoning the wall and heading into town. At the intersection of Franklin and Eighth, they watched a huge fireball explode at the Foothills Gate down the street. Dusky stared at the flaming towers, hearing automatic gunfire and another explosion. The thick wooden and iron gate blew inward, becoming nothing more than shredded metal and burning wood. A white riot car burst through the smoke and flame, gun ports blazing as it spun around to concentrate on the soldiers scrambling for cover.

"Shit! It's Azteca!" Shake cursed from behind them.

Dusky sped up, passing Remy and matching Delva's riot car. "How far?"

"Not too much. Just a couple of more blocks."

"Well, hustle, damn it! We're going to have a hell of a party with Azteca chippin' in!"

Delva nodded and accelerated. Dusky stayed with the riot car, her family bringing up the rear. As promised, three blocks later, Delva slowed down and pulled around the back of an old brick apartment complex. As the vehicles skidded to a halt, a man and a woman piled out of Delva's car, dragging camouflage netting with them. With the Ba'Cho's help they covered the bikes, the vehicles blending into the overgrown yard. The man ducked back into Delva's vehicle, emerging with weapons. The woman waved them toward the complex.

"C'mon! Through here!"

Dusky looked at Delva, eyebrow raised.

"They're chill, Dusk. They can help the *gringa*." He took her forearm, gripping it tightly. "I've gotta get back to the base. It'll be expected."

"Stay alive, dawg. We need you now more than ever."

He nodded and grinned. "I will."

Dusky saw the others waiting by the door with the two strangers and trotted after them. Delva clambered back into his riot car and pulled away.

* * *

"I'm Liz and this is Tank." Liz hustled them through an abandoned apartment. She was an older woman, hair nearly white, with a small, wiry build. Tank took up the rear and looked much like his name. At first glance, he was a bald, muscle-bound jock. Sam blinked at the solid metal spikes sticking out of his cranium in a forest of sharp points. *How old school.* She almost tripped on a broken chair and forced herself to watch where she placed her feet. Trash and broken furniture scattered across the floor. There was just enough light from the dawning sky to illuminate a rat scrounging along a baseboard. Liz led them to a small door under a set of stairs. "Ladder here, folks. Watch out." She opened the door, grabbed a rung set into the wall and swung down into darkness with the ease of familiarity.

Shake and Remy looked at Dusky, who urged them to follow. A staccato of gunfire and another explosion reminded Sam of what was outside. *What the hell is going on out there?* The building rattled. She glanced outside, seeing flames from the gate shoot high enough to be seen over the rooftop of the nearest house. Again the building shook from a distant explosion, and then it was her turn to go down the ladder. Golden light rose to meet her until she was surrounded by it. At the bottom of the ladder, she stepped away to give the others room; Dusky was already halfway down. Sam turned to warily look around. Remy and Shake had split up. They watched Liz bustle about the room, turning on more lights. The basement was large and roomy. All the windows had been boarded up, and Sam couldn't remember if she had seen basement window wells outside or not. Despite the size of the room, it had a cluttered air. Computer parts, books, extra clothing, tools, old dishes and cups vied for space on every conceivable surface. One side of the room held a long table made from old doors and ancient metal filing cabinets. Three sleek and shiny computers rested there, at odds with the destitute appearance elsewhere.

Tank shut and locked the trap door before coming down, Shake and Dusty already awaiting him. Sam was surprised to realize that they had created a lethal triangle around her. No weapons had been drawn, but the tension was thick and their stances indicated that they would quickly quash an attack. Tank lumbered past, setting his rifle down on a coffee table. He gave them a once-over before joining Liz at the computer stations. His hands wove a tale, moving through the air with a grace that belied his rough-and-tumble appearance.

Liz turned to them. "Tank wants the courier to have a seat so we can do a diagnostic on her processor." Sam took a step forward but was blocked by Dusky's arm.

Dusky nodded a chin at Tank. "He's deaf?"

They both smiled back. "No, no. No vocal cords. He can hear just fine."

"Good." Dusky stepped forward and glared into his eyes. "If anything happens to *mi preciada*, you'll live to regret it."

Her growl did all sorts of pleasant things to Sam, reminding her that there was life and love despite the massacres she'd survived to date. Tank gave Dusky a solemn nod, and Sam put her hand on Dusky's shoulder. Dusky turned to her, face softening. "It's okay. I've done this before. It's SOP."

Dusky studied her, a faint smile indicating she remembered their discussion about standard operating procedures on the base the previous afternoon. She nodded and stepped back, but remained within reach. She glanced back at her pack mates. Shake moved to the other side of the room for a different vantage point of the proceedings. Remy turned and sidled off, poking around to see the layout.

Sam settled into the offered chair. Tank's touch was gentle as he thumbed aside the fleshy cover of her data port. With a few hand signals, he indicated something to Liz. Liz retrieved a computer pad and an adapter cable. They behaved much the way a nurse and surgeon would act in an operating room. Handing the plug to Sam, he waited for her to hook herself up. Several minutes passed as he peered at the information flowing across a nearby monitor. He made adjustments, checked the code and typed in the occasional command. Liz accessed a second computer, piggybacking the information on her screen.

Remy returned, making no attempt to lower his voice as he reported to Dusky. "Two bathrooms—one's being used for a film lab. Two bedrooms—one used, one not." Sam watched the two strangers, wondering if they were offended at his reconnaissance, but neither seemed insulted as they continued to putter over their computers. She saw Remy glance at her. "How long are we staying?"

"Don't know. Depends on if and when they can get the data out of her."

"I'll take our gear to the unused bedroom." He moved away at Dusky's nod, gathering their gear.

Tank signed something, and Liz asked, "Do you have the download codes at all?"

Sam refrained from disrupting the cable with a shake of her head, holding herself still. "No, they were sent separately. My contact on the base said she had them."

"Well, no bother. It'll just take a bit longer while we figure it out." Tank added a small datapad to the mix, running it through the main system. A small window popped up on the screen with numbers and letters streaming across it. Liz straightened from her stance hunched over a keypad. "Now we wait. Anybody for breakfast?"

Sam's stomach growled. She felt the blush spreading across her skin as Dusky grinned.

"I'd say so." Dusky put her hand on Sam's shoulder.

Liz retreated to a corner of the room that housed a rudimentary kitchen. Under Shake's watchful eye, she threw together sandwiches, happily chatting with him regardless of being under guard in her own home. Remy set up shop in the corner of the living room and cleaned his pistol. His rifle remained close at hand. Tank retreated to another long table cluttered with electronic equipment. It looked like he was dismantling an old computer to salvage parts. Dusky left Sam's side, disappearing down the hall where Remy said bedrooms and a bathroom were located.

Sam leaned back, glad for the comfortable chair, and closed her eyes. Instead of blessed peace, the sight of soldiers sprawled dead and dying in a corridor forced her to open them again. She glanced at her shoulder, seeing dried blood on her arm. Looking down at herself, she felt a lump grow in her throat. Dusky's shirt was splattered with the blood of people that had either wanted Sam dead or had simply wanted to escape the destruction raining down upon Ritzy's. Dusky returned with a bowl of water and a rag. She sat on a stool and began cleaning the blood from Sam's face and neck. With her emotions so close to the surface, Sam closed her eyes, forcing the horrible visions away as Dusky washed her skin. She felt a moment's trepidation when Dusky dabbed at her right ear, but she was careful not to jostle the cord connected to Sam's port. When Dusky moved past her throat, Sam opened her eyes. "Can I ask you a question?" She peered into one emerald and one silver eye before Dusky returned her gaze to the task at hand, a slight smile on her face.

"Sure."

"Where'd you get the cyberware?" Sam brought up her left hand, fingers tracing the path of four tiny red feathers tattooed on Dusky's right cheekbone. All of the Lichii Ba'Cho had the tattoos, even Delva, though Remy was the only one that had four like Dusky.

"Training accident in the marines. They call it 'friendly fire.'" Dusky finished and set the bowl aside. She moved the stool around until she sat behind Sam.

"You don't look old enough to have been in the marines. You don't even look legal age." Sam wished Dusky would come back into her line of sight, missing her presence until long fingers began to massage her stiff shoulders. *Oh, that makes up for it.* "That feels nice." She groaned as Dusky concentrated on a particularly recalcitrant knot.

Dusky whispered into her ear. "I'm old enough." As Sam shivered, she pulled away, speaking normally. "It's tradition. When a warrior reaches sixteen, he or she participates in the Sun Dance. After healing up, they join the military." She shrugged. "We usually have a get-together during the summer solstice. Have ceremonies, do the dance, welcome home those who've served their time. This year we couldn't."

Sam remembered the talk in the bar. "The Aryans."

"Yeah. Looks like Shake's gonna be a year late."

Across the room, Remy spoke up. He sat just within the range of Sam's vision. "We could always have the ceremony when this is over. No need to wait for next year." He finished cleaning his pistol and began to reassemble it.

"That'll leave only two of us for a year until Delva gets out. And who knows if we can find the others out there. Would that be wise?"

Remy finished and holstered his weapon. "One person ain't gonna make any difference at this rate, Dusk." His eyes settled on Sam. "Will it?"

Sam blinked at him. "You're asking me?" He gave her a simple nod, and she felt a sympathetic squeeze on her shoulder. "Is this a test?" He didn't answer. Sam wondered what she should say. Remy had said some harsh things about her and, even though he'd apologized, she had to wonder if his opinion of her was still so awful. She could put her foot in it and damn herself for all time, making her life miserable if she stayed. "One person does make a difference," she offered. At his nod, she grew bolder. "Still, with only three of you now, his leaving will have an effect. You said it's not always this way?" Again he nodded.

Behind her, Dusky spoke. "It only gets this bad once or twice a year. We've seen more fighting this year than we do most."

"Shake will know that you couldn't weaken your position further by allowing him to go. But he'll still feel held back, not a warrior, not a man." Sam's eyes lit up. "That's it, isn't it? It's what your people do to become adults."

"What would you do?" Remy asked.

She wondered if she would ever get through all of this man's tests. *How many more will there be?* "I'd let him go, do the ceremonies and the dance. When he's healed, enlist him." A warm hand settled on Sam's neck, and she relaxed at the support it conveyed.

"And what would you do, Uncle?"

With a slight quirk to his lips, Remy tilted his head to one side. "I'd do the same." He rose and stretched. "I'm gonna go take a nap, Dusk. Three hours sleep doesn't make it for these old bones." He sauntered down the hall.

"I guess I passed." Sam blushed lightly when Dusky chuckled, not realizing her mutter had been overheard.

"Yeah, I'd say you passed."

CHAPTER TWENTY-TWO

"Report!"

"*Comrade One, all gate control is in our possession. Transferring personnel and equipment into Boise.*"

"*Comrade Two, exterior patrols have turned up a few hundred prisoners of war. We're setting up an internment camp in the fairgrounds.*"

"*Beta One, no appreciable resistance at this time.*"

"*Beta Two, I've got minor skirmishes on the east side of town. Looks like small pockets of soldiers or law enforcement are still active.*"

Shimizu grinned to himself as he heard the news. It had taken over two hours of difficult fighting, but Uncle Sam had been destroyed in Boise, Idaho. This was the first American city to fall to Azteca, and he couldn't be more pleased. When this was over, he'd get one hell of a bonus.

The manager beside him gave praise to his troops. "I want a sweep through the city for hostiles. We need to take care of their resistance before the civilians begin rallying behind them."

Shimizu leaned forward, touching his peer's arm. "We need to find the courier. Canadian citizen Sam Elias."

Nodding, the manager added the order. While his units responded back, Shimizu was hard-pressed not rub his hands together and cackle. It didn't matter if this Elias person was dead or alive; in either case, her processor would be his soon, and God help Uncle Sam when he got his hands on that virus.

* * *

General Dan McAndrews chewed viciously on the end of the stylus as he stared at the satellite maps laid out in front of him. Since losing contact with Boise, his staff had collected all the data they could get their hands on and he'd been in contact with the President. His office at the Mountain Home Air Force Base was large, as befitted his rank, with an ancient mahogany desk and shelves. The desk was currently buried under surveillance and recon maps and reports. The other chairs in his office were occupied by his aides—one on the phone with NASA and one twitching and spasming in that unique dance of the wirelessly connected.

It was a given that Boise had been taken by Azteca. Most of the base itself appeared to be in ruins, and there was severe damage to two of the gates and some damage to the city itself. *Them's the breaks in war.* This was the first time that any of the corporations had made a move on a major American metropolis. *Why the hell are they doing it now?*

The printer on his desk livened up, spitting out more reports and paperwork. The aide on the net spoke, "Here're some numbers from the latest recon, sir. Possible occupancy rates at this point." There was a pause. "It appears that Azteca is sending more shock troopers into the city. Looks like a regular convoy moving up I-84."

McAndrews's face soured. He chewed the stylus with more energy. Waving his hand imperiously at the aide on the phone, he ordered, "Hang up! We need to set up an ambush."

* * *

The morning drifted along in quiet repose. Whatever battle had occurred at the nearby gate had long since subsided, leaving the basement occupants oblivious to the current state of affairs. Dusky had sent Shake off for a nap after he ate; he'd stayed up all night in the bar and needed the rest. Tank continued his salvage mission, graduating from an ancient monitor to a more modern computer deck that he dismantled for parts. Liz elected to crash on the couch, snoring slightly in the flickering light of the television. There wasn't a lot of news to be had; whoever had control of the station was running syndicated talk shows rather than anything pertinent. Dusky cleaned and sharpened the knife she'd used in Ritzy's garage. The soft sound of metal on stone had lulled Sam into sleep.

Dusky finished and slipped the blade into a scabbard at her wrist. Next out was the .45 she'd lent to Sam during the raid. She heard a soft snuffle and glanced at Sam, noticing the deep, even breathing of her slumber. Mi preciada, *will you stay with me? Or will you come to your senses when this* malícia *is over and return to your home?* Her fingers twitched in their desire to reach out and gather Sam into her arms, to hold her forever. Instead, Dusky dropped her gaze and returned her attention to the pistol. *One day at a time, Ba'Cho. One day at a time.* Never had she felt this way for a woman. Never had a woman made such an impact on her within minutes of their meeting. Dusky wasn't sure what had prompted her to invite Sam to join them after the Azteca ambush on the military convoy, but she sent her thanks to the Great Spirit for whatever had spurred her to do so.

The pistol hadn't been fired and was clean. Dusky put it back together, loaded it and returned it to its holster. Next up was the rifle she had liberated from the soldier in the stairwell. She examined the standard issue M22A2. It was the same model as the one she'd discarded on the road outside Boise the day before. With a little credit out, she'd be able to pick up a grenade launcher for it and be back to her original armament. *At least the grenade rounds I have won't go to waste.*

She broke down the rifle, beginning the arduous process of cleaning gunpowder discharge from it, familiarizing herself with the quirks of her new weapon. As she worked, her thoughts drifted back to a love she'd been fortunate enough to witness as a child. The love her parents had held for each other had been legendary among her people. Camilla Three Mountain had been a beautiful young woman; some said Dusky looked just like her. Camilla had been Ice's second wife, the first having died childless in the time before he and Remy had founded the Lichii Ba'Cho. Dusky's childhood memories were filled with her parents' adoration. When Dusky was ten, Camilla had died, her death almost crippling Ice. Remy took over the raising of his nieces, both Dusky and the newborn Camilla, allowing his brother time to heal and refocus. Remy had never married, and the baby ultimately became the property of the entire clan—Camilla had been nursed, spanked and doted on by every woman riding with the Lichii Ba'Cho. Dusky had begun her warrior training in earnest. Ice had never remarried, and now Dusky felt she understood why. Once a love of that magnitude had been experienced, all else was pale imitation. She studied Sam's sleeping face. *What will I do if you go home?* Her heart ached and a lump formed in her throat. She swallowed hard and returned to the rifle. *You won't go. I'll do anything to keep you.* "Anything," she whispered fiercely. Completing the rifle cleanup, she snapped it back together and retrieved her Armalite 44.

Remy entered the room, nodded at Tank and pulled a chair up to Dusky. Sinking into it, he jabbed a chin at the sleeping Sam. "How's it going?"

Dusky gave the computer monitor a quick glance. The small pop-up window still ran permutations, but it appeared most pieces of the decryption phrase had been discovered. "Pretty good. Looks like we're only a couple of numbers short. Should be any time now."

"Good." He watched her work. "How are you, *vida*?"

Dusky smiled and looked up. "Doing good, Uncle." She glanced over at Sam. "You remember my mother?"

"Yes, Dusk."

She shrugged sheepishly, feeling her face heat. "She reminds me of her." Dusky focused her attention on the pistol, not wanting to see Remy's expression. Silence grew between them, and she wondered if he felt disappointment. She saw his craggy hand reach out, taking one of hers, stopping her actions.

"Dusky, you have my blessing."

She broke into a faint smile, finally looking at him. Her one natural eye stung with unshed tears, and she took a deep breath. Turning her palm up, she completed the connection between them, squeezing his hand. "Thank you, Uncle." The moment was lost to a screeching alarm. Sam jolted awake, and both Dusky and Remy jumped to combat readiness.

It took a moment for Dusky to realize the jangling noise came from the decryption program on the computer. The pop-up window blinked, a series of green letters and numbers flashing at her. Tank hustled toward them. Liz rubbed sleep from her eyes and followed. Remy backed away to give them room to work while Tank shut off the alarm and tapped in a series of commands. He signed vigorously and unplugged the small box, inserting it into another computer while Liz translated.

"Tank says we've got the code. We're going to download it now."

Remy reholstered his pistol. "I'll go get Shake."

Dusky nodded, her pistol still in hand. She put it away, grinning at Sam. "Good morning."

"Morning," Sam grumped, a cross look on her face. "Have I told you how much I hate alarm clocks?"

Dusky chuckled. "We don't usually have much need of them."

"Hallelujah," Sam breathed. She sat up carefully. "Yet another good reason to hang out with you."

Dusky ran her fingers through Sam's short hair, straightening the worst of the sleep-tangles at the back.

"You said a terabyte compressed, right?" After Sam nodded, Liz continued. "Okay. This will hold it. We might even be able to crack the encryption on the file itself! Wouldn't that be a hoot?" She cackled as Sam grinned at her, and Dusky wondered where Delva had found these people.

Tank slid a keypad across the table to Sam, pointing at the "enter" button. He nodded, indicating it was all hers. "Okay." Sam settled herself in her chair, finger on the button. She paused as if preparing herself.

Dusky watched her, puzzled at her hesitation. "What does it feel like? Does it hurt?" She sometimes felt phantom pain in her eye and could hardly fathom what it was like to have a data storage unit in her head. *Does it feel wrong somehow to her?*

Sam's mouth pursed as she considered a response. "It feels like my sinuses are really plugged and it suddenly all drains away." She shrugged. "It'll be a relief, but I'll somehow feel hollow in my head, like there's nothing left inside."

Shake had come into the room. "Mythic."

Dusky rolled her eyes at his typical teenaged response as he turned away from the proceedings to search for another sandwich in the kitchen. Looking back at Sam, she was pleased to see her dimple and smiled back. Sam took a deep breath, closed her eyes and pushed the button.

A small bar graph appeared on the monitor, blinking "download in progress." There was a moment as it hung up, but the code breaker had worked, and the graph showed a sliver of green that grew into a solid bar as the information transferred from Sam's storage unit into the hard drive.

Having never seen something like this, Dusky glanced at Remy, who appeared just as mystified. *Seems pretty easy.* She started to debate the option of adding secure data transport to the list of potential jobs for the Lichii Ba'Cho. The gig would be more lucrative than weapons or drugs and far less likely to result in prison time. *I mean, how could you search for an illegal file in someone's head at a cop stop?* Within a minute, the bar had reached the halfway point, marching on, oblivious to the people watching. It slowed at ninety percent, beginning to creep along but still pushing forward. Dusky glanced at Tank and Liz, but they both seemed unperturbed, so she had to assume the lag was normal.

As the counter reached the one hundred percent mark, two things happened. A loud snap threw Dusky's hand from Sam's head. Sam stiffened, her body jerking as if on a string. Acrid ozone filled the air. Simultaneously, the downloading computer crashed. The screen flashed blue once and went dark. The secondary computer Liz had connected abruptly indicated a download in progress and, though the first monitor was black, the power indicator on the deck itself flashed as if it continued working.

"No!" Dusky grabbed the cable connecting Sam to the computer, feeling a jolt of electricity, and yanked it out. Sam stopped convulsing, unconscious. With Shake's and Remy's help, Dusky moved Sam away from the frantically working techs to the couch.

Tank grabbed the first computer's keypad, punching in commands. The second computer completed its download in a quarter of the time it had taken for Sam. The screen flashed blue and blacked out, just as the first. The third computer monitor in the daisy-chained system showed a download in progress. In desperation, Liz yanked its connections before it too could become infected. "It's a fucking virus!" Liz reached for the modem and yanked out the phone lines before the computers could connect to the 'net.

It was too late. The computer plague had begun.

* * *

*(Excerpt, PeepsterNet ChatUp network, Sunday,
5/13/2057, 05:47:52)*

#boise

huskyOWT: Did anybody else hear that? Was that an earthquake? #boise

crv669: What? What's going on? Hear what? #boise

huskyOWT: Thought earthquake. Maybe explosion. Missile overhead a second ago? #boise

LaCaPrints: No way. Nuthin but taters in ID. #boise

crv669: I'm not there. I don't know. #boise

huskyOWT: heard missiles before in Nicaragua. Sounds like 'em. #boise

huskyOWT: SHIT! #boise

372TaTeR: OMG! Someones bombing #boise! #war

LaCaPrints: What? You're shitting me. #boise

DrkRoos: RT 372TaTeR: OMG! Someone's bombing #boise! #war

huskyOWT: Serious. My house is rocking from the noise. That last was by one of the gates. #boise

372TaTeR: At the window. Look at this - *tny.lnk/gu49W* #boise

g3n0c1d3: @372TaTeR: What the hell is that? #boise

crv669: That's a hell of a fireball! RT 372TaTeR At the window. Look at this - *tny.lnk/gu49W* #boise

huskyOWT: Looks like that's the army depot! #Boise

LaCaPrints: WAS the army depot. RT huskyOWT Looks like that's the army depot! #boise

DrkRoos: Gotta be a fuckup. Why bomb bumfuck ID? #boise

372TaTeR: @DrkRoos no FU. Real deal. Bugging out!

CHAPTER TWENTY-THREE

Feel the need for speed? Concerned about security
on the road? We have the bike for you!

The Valdez Special Trike

Three off-road solid wheels give you maximum
stability and the freedom of choice—stay on the
smooth and narrow or head for rougher ground.
The X-Heavy Titanium frame still keeps you light
and maneuverable, and the latest Hyundai mid-size
auto powerplant gives you the power you need to
cruise the highways.

Still not sure?

Check out the dual-mounted M-60 machine guns
that fire 500 belt-fed NATO rounds apiece!

The entire trike is protected by the heaviest Kevlar armor available and includes a targeting computer and QuikSplice between the two M-60s. You'll never miss those nomads or booster gangs should they come gunning for you!

The Valdez Special Trike

Nothing but the best!

(All restrictions apply, must be 21 years old and have legal weapons permit for M-60 attachments, see agent for more details.)

* * *

The major in charge of the Rolling O's fighting wing barked orders at the four other pilots. "All righty then, boys. Coming up on their last known coordinates. Stay sharp and keep your eyes peeled. They couldn't have gotten far." He busied himself at the controls of his copter, an R34 Recluse, rechecking altitude, weapons and location. The ground below rushed by in a blur of desert brown. They would be coming up on I-84 within minutes.

Official reconnaissance and satellite photos had shown the first of four Azteca convoys in the area to be ten vehicles long and heading east for Boise. Government operatives inside Azteca were unable to give any information on manpower. Either this attack was spur of the moment, or their spies hadn't yet breached corporate security enough. The copters came in low over a rise, cutting through the air as they headed west, and the interstate lay before them.

"There they are! Twelve o'clock! Right on the money!" a pilot, Iggy, exclaimed happily.

As reports had stated, ten vehicles headed for them, six of them fully armed riot cars. The remaining four looked to be armored personnel carriers—not much in firepower, but thick-skinned enough to cause difficulties.

The major, known as the Boss, wondered why so few troops were on the road. *There have to be more coming from behind.* Leaving the thought for later, he gave the order. "Let's go, boys! Fire at will! Let's flatline these puppies!" The brass at Mountain Home would have more intel and a new target for them when this group was destroyed.

The five machines swooped toward the lead vehicle, Boss's wingmen coming around to the flanks of the column. Boss opened up with his Walther cannons, the first round exploding too far forward to do any damage. Getting a better range, he fired again. The lead vehicle, a riot car, blew in a brilliant pyrotechnic display. The personnel carrier behind was unable to stop in time and plowed right into the explosion, seriously damaged. A riot car pulled to the left and opened fire on one of the flanking copters as two riot cars from behind roared forward to get into the action. A fireball erupted to the Boss's left, and he heard one of his men say, "They got JC!" The riot car turned toward him and fired a missile. Boss jerked the controls of his Recluse, pulling himself out of the missile's path by mere inches. The wingman on his right fired at the riot car, catching it square on and destroying it.

"Score three for Uncle Sam!"

"And one for the Corps," Boss muttered.

Of the two Corps vehicles that had moved forward, the one on the left fired several rounds at the remaining bird on Boss's left. The radio crackled as he heard, "I'm hit! I'm losing fuel!"

"Pull out, Snoop!" the major ordered. He watched as the pilot hesitated for a second. "That's an order, Lieutenant! Return to base!" he barked and Snoop's copter pulled away.

A flash of white made Boss curse. The riot car before him fired as he hovered dead in the sky. He pulled to the right to avoid another blast and nailed the vehicle with the cannon.

"Four to two!"

"Shaddup, Mac," another voice cut in.

Two riot cars on the right fired simultaneously at the copters near them. The furthest one veered right, avoiding damage, the missile shooting off to detonate in a nearby potato field. The pilot open fired, decimating the car. The other copter wasn't as lucky.

"Dammit! I'm hit, Boss!"

"Pull out, Mac! Follow Snoop!"

"I can't, sir! Controls are sluggish…I'm losing altitude!" the frantic voice said.

"Then unplug, dammit!" barked the major. There was silence and he checked his control panel. The lieutenant was still plugged into his bird. "Unplug, Mac! Get offline!"

"No, sir." The voice was calm. "I'm gonna take these suckers out."

"Mac! That's an order! Offline now!" the major bellowed.

There was no answer as the smoking, wounded copter began to fall. The pilot fought the controls for every inch of airtime, targeting the center of the remaining Azteca formation. The tortured bird shook and shimmied before plummeting down. The resulting crash took out another riot car and an armored personnel carrier, clipping yet a third APC that had been too close.

"Seven to three," the major murmured.

* * *

McAndrews chomped viciously on his stylus, staring down into the amphitheater. Technicians removed the virtual reality helmet and gear from Lt. MacNelson, revealing dead eyes and blood running out his nose and ears. One tech checked for a pulse and shook her head. She gestured for a gurney and the body was removed.

Three of the five pilots remained in their chairs, slaved to their Recluses miles away. "We have a surrender, base," the major's voice said over the speakers. "One riot car and approximately thirty shock troopers from the remaining APCs."

McAndrews punched a button on the console beside him. "You know the drill, Major."

"Yes, sir. No mercy."

"Affirmative. Take 'em out." He paused a moment. "And congratulations."

* * *

What was to become known as the Courier Virus connected to Tank's net provider, pounding against the firewalls and slipping past security programs that had not been inoculated against it. Accessing phone and network lines, it proceeded to spread its message to the main system. From there, it filtered down to thousands of ISP users. Those people too poor to afford wetware—data plugs and CPU processors imbedded in the meat and brains of their bodies—were the lucky ones. Their systems shorted out, but they remained healthy though angry at the disruption. Those physically attached to their equipment through interface cables received a literal shock to their systems, just as Sam had. As one netrunner would state months later, it was "just enough to scramble, not enough to fry."

The Courier Virus burned along every available path, every modem, every wireless network connection. It accessed other providers, telnet computers, old-fashioned bulletin boards, email programs and intranet computers. On and on. It didn't take much time for it to reach the bastions of commerce and government, treating their systems just as viciously as everyone else's.

* * *

"Go!" Shimizu chased bits of data across his desktop, as he tried to keep up with the convoy's progress. *I should have stayed in the war room for this.* He hated the distraction and prepared to flay the idiot who had the audacity to call him through his privacy block.

"Harrelson here, sir. Are you online?"

Shimizu scowled. "Of course I'm online, you idiot! I'm working!"

"Unplug now, sir!"

"Why? Whatever for? This is not a good time, Harrelson!"

"A virus, sir. It's been downloaded into some of our systems. It's just a matter of time—"

"Virus?" Shimizu's eyes narrowed. "Have you run the virus protection proggie we downloaded from that courier?"

"Yes, sir." There was a pause.

"And…?"

"It doesn't protect against this virus, sir! What's infecting our systems is altogether different, something no one has seen before."

Shimizu swore. "Well, fix it, Harrelson. Now!"

"Yes, sir, we're do—"

Everything went black as a shaft of fire seemed to fill Shimizu's vision. He felt his body stiffen and convulse, a burning sensation seizing his muscles, taking control of his body. It was with odd detachment that he saw the white hot flames in his vision were from his data connection—the room itself was dark, the lights out.

Then another blackness swept over him, and he knew nothing more.

CHAPTER TWENTY-FOUR

Two frantic groups moved within the confines of the basement. Liz and Tank worked diligently over the computers, dismantling them to see what kind of physical damage had been done to their core systems. Liz moved the uninfected computer to one side, as if physical separation would make a difference. The Lichii Ba'Cho surrounded the couch where Dusky had settled the unconscious Sam. Frantic, she checked for a pulse, relief flooding through her as she found a steady rhythm. Peeling back Sam's eyelids, she noted the uneven dilation of the pupils. "Concussion." She glanced at Shake. "Get me a wet rag. We need to wake her up." As he dashed off, she edged beneath Sam's body, cuddling her close while Remy adjusted Sam's feet and legs.

"Here you go, Dusky." Shake handed her a wet washcloth.

Dusky used the cool cloth to wash Sam's face. "Hey, *mi preciada*, wake up. Come on. This is no time for sleeping." Turning Sam's head, she dabbed at the irritated skin around the dataport behind her ear. It looked almost like a sunburn; the physical damage coupled with evidence of a concussion worried her. *What did that file do to her?* Several tense moments passed as she jostled and spoke to Sam, Shake and Remy crouching alongside as helpless witnesses. When Sam shifted in Dusky's arms, she gasped before sending a silent prayer to the Great Spirit. "Wake up, *querida*." Sam struggled to open her eyes. They drooped once, twice, and then she blinked, groaning. "How do you feel?"

Sam mumbled her answer. "Like crap." She licked her lips, grimacing.

Dusky closed her eyes, fighting the desire to jump and shout.

Moving slowly, Sam sat up with Dusky's assistance. She rubbed at her temples, squinting at the nomads staring back at her. "What happened?"

Remy studied her. "What do you remember?"

Sam's brow furrowed. "I don't know. Did I fall asleep?" She felt for the port, finding herself offline. "Did we get the file?" She looked at Dusky in confusion. "What am I doing over here? Why can't I remember the download?" She peered past the Ba'Cho at Liz and Tank working on the machines. "What happened?"

Dusky took Sam's hand. "Calm down, you're okay." She brushed a hand through Sam's hair. "Whatever you carried caused their system to crash. There was some sort of electrical feedback through the interface cable. I disconnected you and brought you over here."

Staring, Sam repeated Dusky's words. "Caused it to crash?"

Liz overheard and looked up. "You were carrying a virus. It infected two of our decks and made it to an outside line."

"Well, I guess that explains why Uncle Sam didn't want it." Remy rose from his squat and looked at the others. "Question is, if they knew what she was carrying, why'd they set up an escort for her in the first place?"

"And a poor one, at that." Dusky's eyes narrowed.

Shake shrugged. "Maybe they didn't find out until she was already on her way here."

Dusky scowled. "Maybe they didn't want her to reach Boise. If that virus had gotten into Azteca hands first..."

"Uncle Sam would win the war," Shake finished, eyes wide.

"Well, Uncle Sam must have the virus protection proggie to control it, then," Liz growled in exasperation. Tank's hands flew in intricate patterns and her scowl deepened.

"What'd he say?" Sam asked.

"He says not necessarily. Otherwise they wouldn't have had a problem with you downloading to their system in the first place."

"True." Sam rubbed her right temple. "If they already had the virus protection software, they could have had me download into a quarantined system and taken care of it themselves."

"Wait a minute." Dusky stood and paced the room. "Canada GovMin sent a courier to Uncle Sam with a virus... so Azteca could capture it? But Uncle Sam doesn't have the program to stop it from infecting their computers? We're talking major *malícia* here, on a fucking global scale!"

Tank signed again and Liz interpreted. "That about covers it."

Sam caught Dusky's eye. "*Malícia?*"

"Double-dealing."

"Oh." She sat back against the couch, closing her eyes.

"Oh, no, *preciada*." Dusky sat beside her, brushing Sam's bangs away from her eyes. "You have to stay awake for a while. That jolt gave you a concussion."

Sam opened her eyes. "It did?" At Dusky's acknowledging nod, she groaned and closed her eyes again. "No wonder my head hurts so much."

"I've got some 'dorphs in my bag." Shake made a move to go back to the spare room but was stopped by Remy's outstretched hand.

"How long we staying, Dusk?"

Dusky frowned and shrugged. "We should wait until the heat's off outside. We might have a better chance of getting out now that Azteca is mucking things up." Despite herself, she yawned.

"You need to relax for a bit. Let's wait until nightfall?"

Dusky considered Remy's suggestion and nodded. "Sounds good."

"You and your *señorita* go back into the spare room. We'll keep an eye on things here." At Dusky's blank look, he raised an eyebrow and spoke with an air of innocence. "She needs something to take care of her headache."

Shake snickered and turned away. Dusky smirked, the grin widening at Sam's blush. *Puta to señorita in less than twenty-four. Will wonders never cease?* "Okay, Uncle, it's a deal." She rose from the couch and pulled Sam to her feet. "C'mon, *preciada*, let's take care of your headache."

The power went out.

Muffled curses came from Shake and Liz. Dusky's infrared option on her cyberoptic kicked in and she saw all the room's occupants. Her hand settled on her pistol as Liz groped her way across the room.

"Everybody stay put." Liz reached a closet and opened its door. She fiddled with something inside. A motor hummed to life, and a few lights came back on. "Generator for emergencies," she said with a grin, shutting the door. "Brownouts are a bitch."

Tank nodded and turned back to his computers. Remy settled down on the couch and pulled out a knife and stone. Liz dusted off her hands and went back to the computer station, Shake following to watch the technicians work. Dusky gave the room a final scan before squeezing Sam's hand. "Let's go, *preciada*. I'll check Shake's bags for the 'dorphs." She led Sam out of the room.

* * *

With the power grid down, further infection was impossible. That didn't negate its danger. The major concern now, especially in larger cities and towns, was Man. As power failed in Seattle, Portland, Tacoma and Lewiston, the darker element reached out from their homes. With no Internet or video to numb their minds, no way to 'wave a snack or keep beer cold, with some people suffering from the repercussions of being online at the time the virus spread through the system, what else was there to do but stir things up? Gang wars flared, the downtrodden took their chance to better their lives and neighbors long held in check by civilization resorted to vigilantism to right the perceived wrongs. As darkness settled over their communities, it would only get worse.

The virus reached beyond the Pacific Northwest. It diligently propagated itself, spreading and spreading and spreading...

CHAPTER TWENTY-FIVE

Sam sank onto the mattress in the spare room. Her head pounded, and she could barely keep her eyes open. A single light over the door gave dim illumination, stabbing brittle fragments into her skull and compounding the pain. She kept her eyes narrowed to slits as she watched Dusky rummage in Shake's gear. Finding what she needed, Dusky approached Sam and sat beside her. "How are you feeling? Any nausea?"

"No. I don't think so." Dusky brushed Sam's hair aside. Sam felt the pressure at the base of her neck as Dusky applied the endorphin patch at the hairline. "Just a splitting headache. My port feels a little weird…" It suddenly occurred to her that this incident might have burned out her processor, and her stomach did a slow roll. *I can't afford a replacement. What if there's more damage than just wetware?*

Dusky's callused hands guided her head to one side. "Looks a little red, like a sunburn, but that's all." She ran her hand down Sam's spine, lightly rubbing. "We'll have it looked at when this is over. I know a decent ripperdoc in Tacoma who's good with processors."

"Great." The pain in Sam's head began to abate, the 'dorphs coursing through her system. She sighed and slumped as the worst of the throbbing faded. Soon the dull ache would disappear for a short time. Her sudden fears did more than enough to compensate for the loss.

"Better?"

"Yeah. Much." Sam gave a half-hearted thumbs-up.

Dusky cocked her head, studying her. "What's wrong?"

Sam took a moment to marshal her thoughts, not wanting to put her concern into words for fear of making them substantial. "What if it did more than just give me a jolt?"

"What do you mean?"

She reached up, lightly caressing the irritated skin around her port. *Does it feel warm, or is that just my paranoia?* "What if it destroyed my processor? What if it caused brain damage?" Her stomach did a complicated series of gymnastics as she looked away, trying to remember where the data storage and CPU were placed in her head. If she recalled the area, she might ascertain if those brain functions had changed.

Before she developed a serious panic attack, Dusky took her chin between her thumb and forefinger, grabbing her attention. "It didn't."

"You can't know that."

"I can."

Dusky's eyes were calm, exuding a quiet strength. Sam wanted so badly to believe but couldn't quite bring herself to do so. She felt tears sting her eyes. "How do you know?"

Dusky loosened her grip, running her thumb along Sam's jawline. "You're walking, you're talking. You hear what I say and can comprehend it, right?" At Sam's silent nod, Dusky chucked her chin. "Processors like yours usually hook into the temporal lobe, near the auditory cortex. If you can hear me and can process my speech, you should be fine."

Dumbfounded, Sam stared at her. Her romantic vid-based image of the wild American Indian biker-nomad took a hard blow, but Dusky was right. She took a deep breath, trying to calm herself as Dusky continued speaking.

"You have a possible concussion, which meant things overheated in there, caused enough of an electrical feedback to bruise the brain tissue around the processor." She pulled away from Sam. "Once we get out of here, we'll have you looked over just in case, but I don't think you have anything to worry about."

Sam watched as Dusky stood and returned to the gear, reconciling her fictional misconceptions of gangster education with reality. She'd been so caught up in the flight and gun battles that the situation had almost become like any number of vintage vids she'd viewed in her youth. "At the very least, it probably burnt out my CPU."

"We'll replace it."

The matter-of-fact comment made Sam blink. "Do you know how much they cost?"

Dusky looked back at her, a grin on her face. "Don't worry about it. If it helps, you can work on our bikes to pay it off."

Sam felt a sense of hope for the first time since this mess had started. As much as she wanted to stay with Dusky and the Lichii Ba'Cho, she hadn't been able to conceive the possibility. The dream of romantic bliss on the road had eluded her in light of the fact that she knew absolutely nothing real of their lifestyle—as was apparent by her surprise at Dusky's knowledge of wetware—and had no useful value in return. All this time she did have something to bring to the table, a skill set for which the nomads with their depleted population had a use.

"Think you could eat some?" Dusky held up a military ration.

Sam tilted her head to one side, noting her stomach had settled with her fears. "I could give it a go." Her stomach agreed with a grumble, and she felt a slight smile curve her lips.

Dusky chuckled. She sat next to Sam and handed her the food. "Take it slow, *preciada*."

"Thanks." Sam opened the pouch and waited for the heating element to do its job before eating. She paid close attention to her stomach, not wanting to waste the pack's dwindling resources, and was mildly pleased to note it tendered no complaints. While they ate, she envisioned a new future, a more realistic one where she was given access to all the combustion engines she wanted and traveled the American countryside with a beautiful, sexy woman. *If I can keep my processor and storage unit, I can volunteer to run data too.* The daydream felt comfortable, real, and Sam finished her lunch with a renewed sense of promise.

Dusky finished at the same time and gathered their trash together, setting it on the nightstand. Sam scooted more fully onto the bed, sitting on her knees with her back to the headboard. She patted the mattress in front of her. "Sit here." She smiled at Dusky's raised eyebrow. "Your uncle said you needed to relax. Nothing more relaxing than a back massage. I come from a long family line of master masseuses."

"Really?" Dusky grinned. "Looks like I got a pretty good deal when I picked you up." She climbed onto the bed, sitting in front of Sam.

Sam tapped Dusky on the shoulder. "The shirt's got to go." She wiggled her eyebrows at Dusky's chuckle. "Otherwise, you won't get the full…uh…'benefits.'"

Dusky did as she was told, tossing the garment to the foot of the bed. "Anything else?"

"Well, yeah. But that can wait until later." Smirking over her shoulder, Dusky pulled her thick hair forward out of Sam's way. Sam dug her fingers into Dusky's shoulders and neck, meeting stiff resistance. "My God! These are rocks, not shoulders!" Dusky's only answer was a dry chuckle. Sam lightened her touch, deciding she needed to work her way down through the layers. Dusky's head sagged in contentment, and Sam smiled as she worked.

"So, tell me about Sam, master masseuse."

Sam pursed her lips. "Not much to tell, really. My life hasn't been near as exciting as yours." She stroked her thumbs up Dusky's spine, bracketing it, enjoying the slight moan she overheard. "I'm a poor little rich girl, a corpsbrat. Only child, private schools, tutors, you know."

"How'd a corpsbrat end up a courier? That's an independent career. Didn't want follow in your parents' footsteps?"

Sam shrugged slightly though Dusky couldn't see it. She concentrated on a knot deep in Dusky's right shoulder. "My folks had been assigned to the Panama embassy. They were killed in a terrorist strike during the Food Riots of '41."

Dusky stilled Sam's hand with hers as she turned slightly. "I'm sorry," she said in all seriousness. "Losing a parent is never easy, especially as a child."

Shrugging again, Sam accompanied it with a slight smile. "Thanks. It's okay, though. That was years ago." She squeezed Dusky's shoulder lightly before pulling away from the hand that held her. Dusky took the hint and allowed Sam to continue. "Anyway, I ended up running away from the corps orphanage. Spent a few years on the streets, doing what streetkids do." Her hands moved lower, working beneath the shoulder blades. "About three years ago, a fixer found me. Said I had some money coming to me from the corporation my parents had worked for. After giving him a cut for locating me, I had enough for a processor and storage unit." Sam heard a small groan as she applied pressure to the muscles and grinned. "Been running data ever since. What about you?"

"What about me?"

Sam laughed. "Okay. For starters, tell me about the tattoos."

"Oh." The muscles beneath Sam's hand moved as Dusky reached up to caress the tiny feather tattoos at the corner of her right eye. "They represent belonging and rank in the tribe."

"That's it?"

Dusky huffed a silent chuckle. "The first is given on a baby's name day to signify they belong to the tribe. The second is for reaching adulthood. The third is for completion of military service. And the fourth is reserved for those who reach some sort of position in the clan."

Sam frowned, considering her discussion with Dusky and Remy earlier in the day. "But—Shake's got two and you said he hasn't been through the ceremony yet."

"Yeah, but we've seen pretty heavy fighting this year. He's made several kills on his own. That alone makes him an adult and warrior in the clan. The ceremony is just—an acknowledgment of the fact."

Sam's hands stroked down to Dusky's lower back, her mind shying away from the idea of Shake collecting scalps like American Indians from two hundred years ago. "Do all of your people join the military?"

"No." Dusky shook her dark head. "It depends on the individual. Those that don't want to be warriors don't do the Sun Dance or enter the military. Everyone's considered adult at sixteen. Instead of military service, they apprentice as children in various ways—mechanics, electronics, things like that. They get their third tat when they've reached some sort of proficiency in their chosen field."

Returning her attention to Dusky's shoulders, Sam was pleased to note the growing pliancy there. "You and Remy have the same number of feathers. Elders equal leaders?" She dug firmly into the muscles.

Dusky moaned. "God, this feels good." It took her several moments to return to the conversation. "When my father was killed, it put me in charge. When we have the ceremony for Shake, I'll have another tat added."

Sam leaned forward, bringing her lips close to Dusky's left ear. "If I stay with you, do I get tattooed as well?" She grinned as a shiver ran through the body beneath her hands.

"Um, if you want to. It would help to integrate you into the pack." Dusky paused, leaning back into Sam. Her next words were a whisper. "Will you stay?"

Sam smiled fondly at the hesitant tone. For all Dusky's arrogance and attitude, Sam had somehow unlocked the core of the woman rather than the leader. It was a gift she didn't think Dusky had realized she'd bestowed, giving Sam a power over her she might not appreciate in the future. As much as Sam wanted to jump at the chance to remain with Dusky, she had to consider the possible repercussions. Sure, she could be a happy little grease monkey, playing house with this strong, gorgeous woman, but how long would it last if Dusky didn't understand what had happened between them?

She didn't speak as she varied her touch between light caresses and strong kneading. What had happened between them the night before had gone beyond anything Sam had ever experienced with anyone else. Dusky had touched her in a way no other ever had. *Do I touch her in the same way?* She leaned forward to whisper in Dusky's ear. "I haven't decided yet." She sat back, her lighter skinned hands playing across the darker tone of Dusky's back. "There's something I need to know before I can."

Dusky visibly braced herself, making Sam love her all the more. "What?"

Sam leaned forward again, her words breathing into Dusky's ear. "Will you give yourself to me like I gave myself to you?" Dusky froze, and Sam sat back, continuing the massage as she gave Dusky time to think. She suspected that Dusky had been groomed to take over for her father, else Remy would have been running the show at Sam's first meeting with them. A lifetime of learning to lead, of being in constant control of self and family had to take its toll. Though Sam couldn't help her feelings, she knew that they would crash and burn in a brilliant blaze of fire if Dusky didn't make the conscious choice to let go of that control.

"Everything," Dusky whispered.

"What?" Sam's hands stilled.

Dusky cleared her throat. In a louder voice, she said, "I'll give you everything."

Unshed tears stung Sam's eyes, tears of relief. She leaned forward again, hands moving down to caress Dusky's upper arms. "I don't want everything, love," she whispered fiercely. "I just want you."

"You have me."

Sam rose up on her knees and leaned against Dusky's strong back. Her left hand traced featherlight patterns across Dusky's shoulder and neck, grasping her chin and tilting her head for a kiss. Their lips met with the same hunger that she was becoming accustomed to, a ravenous desire, never quenched. Her lips parted and she felt a hand in her hair, pressing her into the kiss. She growled into Dusky's mouth, a surge of fire running through her system. Sliding her hand along Dusky's arm, she pulled the hand away from her head, bringing it down and firmly pressing it against Dusky's thigh. She pulled away from the kiss, ignoring her lover's groan of loss. "No. Give yourself to me."

Dusky bit her lower lip, eyes uncertain. When she nodded, Sam rewarded her with a soul-searing kiss. She released Dusky's hand, sliding up Dusky's body, teasing sensitive skin. Goose bumps followed in the wake of her touch, and Dusky shivered. Sam stroked across the firm abdomen, moving up until her thumb traced the swell of a breast. "You're so beautiful." She cupped the breast, her thumb barely brushing the nipple. Her free hand caressed past Dusky's ribs, down the hip and along the stretch of leather-clad thigh. "I dreamt of you that first night. Dreamt of having you, of taking you."

Moaning, Dusky leaned her head back, cradled in Sam's hold. Her entire body trembled, and Sam nipped at the lithe neck, noting Dusky's clenched fists as she fought her natural instinct to take over. Sam felt rather than heard Dusky's growl, saw the rapid rise and fall of her breasts. She brushed Dusky's swollen nipple, harder this time, and relished her own arousal as it burned through her, knowing it seared Dusky as well. "Do you want me to take you?" She bit down on Dusky's shoulder at the same time as she pinched the captured nipple, rolling it between her thumb and forefinger. Dusky arched into the rough touch, gasping, the sight and sound so erotic that Sam felt herself soak her underwear. She remembered Dusky demanding an answer last night and repeated it. "What do you want?"

There was no answer. From her vantage point, Sam saw a faint wry grin touch Dusky's lips. *Paybacks are a bitch, sweetheart.* Sam pinched the nipple in her grasp, giving Dusky's breast a firm squeeze. Her other hand fumbled with the catch of Dusky's pants. "What do you want?"

Panting, Dusky found her voice. "Take me."

Sam's fingers slipped beneath the waistband of Dusky's leathers as she complied.

CHAPTER TWENTY-SIX

"All right, I want everything in position by oh three hundred," McAndrews growled to one of his aides.

His aide added the order to his datapad. "Yes, sir. I'll have the message encrypted and sent out."

The general chewed on the ever-present stylus. *Damn, what I wouldn't give for a cigarette!* Two lanterns lit his office since the electricity had been rendered useless. In place of his phone was a battery-powered field unit, an archaic piece of equipment that had long ago been abandoned in favor of the newfangled contraptions of the twenty-first century. "Thank God, Uncle Sam doesn't throw anything away."

"Sir?" the aide asked.

McAndrews looked up sharply. "Nothing. Talking to myself. It's called senility."

"Yes, sir."

He sighed and removed the stylus from his teeth. "We attack at dawn. Make sure the proper attack codes get out there." He turned toward the window, watching dusk fall. "Damn, I hate shortwave radios."

* * *

The smell of food beckoned them from their haven. As darkness fell, Sam and Dusky returned to the living area, arms around each other's waists. Remy sat at the kitchen table, peeling potatoes as if all grizzled Indians with fetish-braided beards did so. Liz sliced them and set them to frying on a propane camp stove. Tank still worked on his precious computers, though he'd apparently decided that they weren't worth the effort to fix. The two that had been infected were now at his other workstation where he dismantled them for future salvage.

Shake peered at a book as he sat on the couch. He glanced up and grinned, winking at Dusky. "You relaxed now?"

"Very." She smiled rakishly and squeezed Sam's waist. There was an answering hug and a faint blush tinted Sam's fair skin. Dusky's smile softened as she imagined small feather tattoos on Sam's face. *Mine.*

"It's getting on toward dark, Dusk." Remy looked up from his peeler. "Figured out what we're going to do, yet?"

Dusky regretfully moved away from her *preciada*. She ran her hand through her hair. "It looked like a lot of damage to that gate closest to us. I figure our chances are pretty good getting out that way." She settled onto a chair, leaning elbows on knees. "Has there been any word from the outside?"

Shake, Tank and Sam moved toward the conversation. Sam stood behind Dusky, Tank pulled up a third chair and straddled it, and Shake leaned against the counter.

Liz stirred the contents of the frypan with a spatula. "Actually, we were able to pick up a little bit from a shortwave we keep for emergencies. Can't pick up much outside of Boise, but we've gotten several reports from inside the city." She adjusted the flame and covered the pan, turning around to face them. "Apparently, Azteca attacked from two sides—this gate got the worst of the assault. No others were messed with."

"There's rioting, of course. Looting," Remy continued. "It'll be getting more violent once the sun goes down. Don't know how many of Uncle Sam's people made it through the attack. Not many, I suspect."

Dusky thought of Delva, seeing solemn understanding from Remy and Shake.

Tank's hands began their dance and Shake stared. Liz said, "At least we're in a good location. Not many people will be looting houses yet. Most of the violent stuff's going to happen outside of the residential areas for now."

"True." Dusky chewed over the scanty information. *I've got to get* mi preciada *out of the city and away from both factions.* One decently damaged gate and lots of rioting in the streets to keep Azteca and the army distracted were the ticket. "And nothing from outside?"

Liz blew out a breath and scrubbed at her face. "Not really. I've gotten some garbled stuff. It was hard to understand." She brushed white hair out of her eyes. "We're not the only ones without power. I think it's pretty widespread. That virus took a lot of systems down, Uncle's and Corps' too."

Remy finished and set the peeler down. He rose and went to the sink to rinse his hands. "You know that Uncle Sam ain't going to let this stand. They're going to take the city back, even if it's in pieces."

Tank and Dusky both nodded in agreement. "It's just a matter of time before they set up some form of communication and get troops in place." Dusky thought for a moment. "Probably dawn tomorrow at the latest. That should give them enough time to do something about it. And," she offered with a glance at her uncle, "if I know Azteca, reinforcements have been pouring into town."

Remy nodded.

Dusky sighed and leaned back into Sam's gentle caress on her shoulders. "Let's bail late at night, early morning, before

Uncle Sam has a chance to attack. If we make it out, their attack will help cover our tracks."

"Sounds good," Shake said. "What about Delva?"

"He's a grown man. He can take care of himself." Dusky scowled, wishing she could do something about their lost man. There weren't enough Lichii Ba'Cho around anymore to throw away. "If he's made it this far, he should be okay. He'll meet up with us when he can." She looked Liz and Tank over in speculation. "You two wanna chip in with us?"

Liz's eyebrows raised in surprise at the invitation. "Um…I don't know." She glanced at Tank. "We'll have to talk about it."

Dusky nodded. "Let me know before we leave. You two are good in a firefight. We could use you." She stood and stretched. "Now where's this shortwave radio you're talking about?"

* * *

Delva huddled in the basement of a house on the north side. Surrounding him were what was left of his platoon. Fifteen had made it through the bombing and subsequent battles, falling back to regroup in the house of someone's vacationing parents.

"Dammit! I say we cut and run! Corps ain't gonna give a shit!" said one man.

"No way! I'm no coward!" a woman responded.

This verbal battle had lasted far longer than any firefight in which they'd been involved. Their superior officers and non-coms were dead. Now they drifted with no direction.

"What do you say, featherhead? You outrank us all at this point."

Delva grabbed the questioner by the throat, lifting him as he stood until the man's toes dangled above the concrete floor. "First, I say that my name is Featherman, and don't you forget it." At the man's strangled agreement, Delva released him, letting him drop to the ground with a thump. He looked around the basement, watching wary eyes study him. "Second, I say we killfile two scripts with one proggie. Let's get out of the city and hook up with Uncle Sam at Mountain Home." There was a muttered round of agreement and Delva squatted again. Time to make some plans.

* * *

Darkness fell over the country. A thick blanket of chaos covered half the United States, stretching from the virus's origin in Boise, Idaho, to Colorado, Texas and almost to the Great Lakes. There were vague maunderings about the situation on East Coast news programs, but the urgency of it was lost on them—those not yet affected lacked comprehension of the danger, suffered an inability to understand the true extent of the virus. No news was good news, and no news was making its way from the now-darkened country. Nor was the United States the only country suffering. Large portions of South and Latin America had been affected, the virus having found its way through corporation and governmental computers to Uncle Sam's allies. In Europe, Paris burned and the Pope was unable to give comforting words to his worldwide flock.

Some countries appeared unaffected. Canada, despite its physical proximity, was the only bastion of light and civilization on the North American continent. Australia, India, the British Isles, South Africa, Japan, a few other countries scattered in the Eastern bloc. Somehow, firewalls had been erected in the cyber world there, the virus crashing uselessly against them. Space stations watching the spread of diseased bits and bytes saw whole sections of the world turn dark, their radios no longer able to reach senior administrators to warn them.

The virus wasn't particular. As long as there was a path of least resistance, room to multiply, it did—washing uselessly up against the barriers that had been erected in its path, rampaging on like a wild river when successfully diverted to other places.

CHAPTER TWENTY-SEVEN

(Two minute video clip, 'Net Sales Net,' Artillery Edition, 5/Noel4/Rachid057)

Noel: Now here's a nice little number—the Milkor MGL-MK1 40mm.

Rachid: Looks damned lethal, Noel! What is it exactly?

Noel: This baby is a six-shot semiautomatic grenade launcher. *(Picks up weapon and holds it for camera close-up.)* This baby provides greater firepower to the grenadier enthusiast and is a hit with light military units and riot police.

Rachid: Wow! Tell us more.

Noel: Originally developed and manufactured in South Africa in the last century, it's been used to quell many an uprising over the last eighty years. Comes with a folding stock for greater firing stability *(folds stock out and back)* and utilizes the time-worn revolver cartridge *(opens cartridge to show chamber)*. With this little number, you can fire six shots in three seconds and cover a twenty-by-sixty-meter area. *(Slaps cartridge closed.)*

Rachid: *(Picks up a grenade round.)* And it fires these, right?

Noel: Right! You can choose between smoke, gas or incendiary rounds. All of them have been used at one point or another in over thirty countries. They even make low pressure rounds for less lethal applications.

Rachid: Now, you said this is used by light military and riot police. Why should our viewers purchase one for home defense?

Noel: The day is coming when the shit will hit the fan, Rachid, and there's been plenty of unrest all over the world. I've got three of these guys stashed around my home. The last thing I want is for a terrorist cell to destroy the infrastructure, but if it happens, I'll be prepared to defend me and mine against mob rule.

* * *

Sam and Dusky helped Liz clean up after the meal. Tank returned to his beloved computers. Shake and Remy went to the back room to gather their gear for the coming assault on the gate.

Dusky was currently doing her "Big Bad Pack Leader" act and hadn't spoken more than two words. That was okay with Sam; she understood the situation needed a strong, concise person in charge, and Dusky was that person. Sam had made her point earlier in the bedroom and would do so again in the future. Breaking the silence, she looked at Liz. "So, how long have you and Tank been together?"

"About seven years." Liz handed her a foil-wrapped package to put into the refrigerator. "I came up from LaCa, searching for this badass hacker who had messed with my friends." A small smile crossed her face, and she chuckled. "It was love at first sight."

"Really?"

"No." Liz laughed again. "Though he seemed to think so. I sure as hell didn't. I just wanted to mess up his deck and go home." She shrugged. "Couldn't get past his security."

Tank rapped on the table to get her attention, signing with a grin.

"Yeah, yeah." Liz waved him off. "He says he had to do something to keep me coming back. Well, it worked!" Finishing with their task, she wiped her hands on a towel and approached the large man. "Next thing I know, I'm moving in with him and becoming his personal techie."

Dusky sprawled on the couch, and Sam perched on the arm of it next to her. A possessive arm draped across Sam's thigh, the hand caressing her kneecap. Sam ran her fingers through Dusky's hair.

"Do you think you'll come with us?" Sam asked the couple.

Tank and Liz looked at each other. "I guess it really depends on this virus. If it ain't too bad, there's no reason we can't continue on here."

"And if it is?" Dusky drawled, watching them steadily.

"Well, then—" Liz froze at the sound of a door slamming upstairs.

Dusky shot out of her seat, pistol drawn. Remy and Shake silently entered from the hallway. With a grace and silence that belied his size, Tank stood and flowed to the ladder, picking up his rifle as he passed the coffee table. Sam heard floorboards creak above as the intruder walked across the room. Whoever it was wasn't being particularly discreet about it. She followed the person's progress with her eyes, matching the noise to the shuffling location as she backed away from potential flashpoint at the ladder. The footsteps stopped at the trapdoor. Tank took the safety off of the rifle and brought it up to his shoulder, sighting upward. Sam felt a

.45 pressed into her palm. Dusky guided Sam to stand behind her. Glancing around, Sam saw Liz holding a massive rifle, one that could easily have been referred to as an "elephant" gun in days of yore. Shake and Remy were positioned to triangulate their fire with Tank's.

There came a soft rapping on the door above, a staccato of sound that varied and lasted for nearly a minute.

Tank grinned and brought his rifle down, setting it against the wall before surging up the ladder. Liz smiled. At Dusky's sharp glance, she held up a hand and lowered the monstrous rifle. "It's okay. It's a friend."

The Lichii Ba'Cho slowly relaxed their stances but didn't put their weapons away. Tank unlocked the door and scrambled down. Seconds later, another large man climbed into the room.

"Delva!" Sam exclaimed.

The big nomad grinned, hands held away from his body. "Well, who the hell did you expect?"

* * *

It was nearly three in the morning when everything was ready. Dusky stood guard with the others as Sam, Tank and Liz finished packing the couple's things into Delva's riot car. Further out in the lot, hidden from normal eyesight, were four soldiers—Delva's fire team. Dusky had no trouble keeping an eye on them with her infrared optics. Two other teams had already moved into position near the Northern Gate, preparing for attack. According to Delva, these were the last of Uncle Sam's troops in the city, the last of his company. Sam's survival lay in the hands of soldiers that had been out for Sam's blood less than a day before. Dusky didn't trust them.

Delva hadn't brought good news. As Uncle Sam and Azteca took out their frustrations upon each other, Boise had become a bloodbath. The only safe place to be was elsewhere.

There weren't enough Azteca personnel to yet hold the city easily, and Uncle Sam would soon throw its hefty weight into the ring to regain ground. It was a sure bet. The downtown area glowed red behind Dusky from fires started during the rioting and looting. Even without additional cybernetic enhancements she smelled smoke and blood, heard angry voices and gunfire. Soon that fury would threaten nearby residences until it engulfed the whole city.

Sam came to her, speaking softly. "We're ready to roll."

Dusky forced herself not to yip in relief. Instead she nodded and looked at Remy and Shake. The younger man was less inclined toward self-control and withered under Remy's glare after he voiced his joy. Without a word, he gave his family a sheepish shrug and mounted his motorcycle. Liz and Tank strapped themselves into the riot car. It roared to life, echoed by the sound of bikes, probably scaring the civilians cowering in the surrounding apartments and homes. *Good. Keep hiding under the beds, sheople.*

Delva trotted over. "Give us a few minutes to get there. We're on foot. The riot car has better armor—it comes behind us and you three behind it."

Nodding in agreement, Dusky kick-started her bike. Delva jogged away, calling his fire team together. She watched the five soldiers move north. With a smile of reassurance, she helped Sam climb onto the bike behind her. She put the .45 back into Sam's hands. "Don't fail to use this if you need it."

Sam swallowed. "I won't." She gripped the pistol tightly and laid it along her right thigh. Her other arm wrapped tightly about Dusky's waist, and Dusky felt Sam lean her head between her shoulders.

Dusky steered her motorcycle toward the riot car. When Tank opened the window, she glanced in at the two of them. "Ready to go?" He nodded. "Okay then. Let's do it. Move slow; we have to give Delva a head start. You're in the lead."

Tank gave another nod and rolled up the window. As he pulled away, Shake and Remy flanked the riot car with Dusky bringing up the rear.

* * *

Delva paused his team a block away from the gate. He sent a man to either side, signaling the two other teams in hiding. One of the two gate towers had completely burned to the ground during the Azteca attack the day before. The other tower was burnt so badly, its usefulness was hardly an issue. A hastily erected guard shack had been set up to the right of the gate, in front of the decimated tower. Two machine gun nests had been built on either side of the road. Aside from the manning of the machine guns, there appeared to be four Azteca shock troopers hanging out in front of the wire contraption that had been placed across the road.

The fire team to his right, B Team, swung in a hair earlier than the one on his left, A Team. Within seconds, the machine gun nest on the right belched fire as it exploded. The shock troopers in the open dived for cover. Another explosion occurred to the left, but the grenade hadn't landed in the sweet spot. The gunner there remained uninjured. After a moment of confusion, he opened fire on A Team.

Delva cursed as two soldiers from A Team fell to the ground in a spray of bullets. The three remaining members of A split up. One dodged right, firing his rifle and nailing two of the shock troopers who'd found insufficient cover. As the middle soldier sprayed rounds at the machine gun nest, his buddy went to the left and tossed a grenade into the hole. The nest exploded in flame and screams as bodies flew from within. The two remaining shock troopers made it to the relative safety of the machine gun nest on the right. They were as surprised as Delva to discover that the weapon remained in good firing condition, having suffered little damage from the explosive round. One of the troopers laughed and opened fire on B Team. Three more of Delva's soldiers danced as the rounds perforated their bodies. The other two hit the ground. One tossed another grenade into the nest, blowing the entire thing up for the second time.

The three remaining members of A Team reached the gate to discover two more machine gun positions on the other side. Alerted by the noise of the battle behind them, the troopers outside the wall had hastily reversed their positions. A Team dashed around the corner of the ruined tower, one of them receiving a rash of bullets in his chest for his troubles. His remaining friends turned back, diving into the destroyed machine gun nest on the left. After a quick conference and an examination of the machine gun, they burst from cover, making a break for the gate. One fired the appropriated machine gun, the other his rifle until they got within sight of the nest on the other side. The second soldier fired a grenade into the position, whooping as it took the nest out. Their joy didn't last long, however, as the second machine gun outside the gate cut them down.

* * *

"Sir!" The aide rushed into the makeshift office.

"What, Captain? We attack in less than an hour. What else is there?" McAndrews growled, looking up from the city map he studied. The ever-present stylus moved furiously around between his teeth.

"There's fighting at one of the gates, sir! Explosions, gunfire."

The general stopped chewing and blinked. "Any idea who it is?"

"No, sir. We haven't gotten an ID, yet. Whoever it is is giving Azteca hell, though, sir."

"Show me which gate!" McAndrews ordered. The aide moved forward and pointed out the position. The general studied the map, eyes narrowed, his stylus moving. "Everything's in place?"

"Yes, sir."

With a satisfied nod, he removed the stylus and pursed his lips. "Roust the men. We attack in five minutes." As the aide blinked at him, he barked, "Now, man!"

"Y...Y...Yes, sir!" The captain ran out of the room. "Let's kick some Corporation butt."

* * *

Now aware of the danger lying outside the gates, the remaining members of A Team carefully moved along the wall toward the half-ruined tower. They stopped at the machine gun nest along the way, only to be disappointed that the weapon was useless. Delva looked behind him and saw the approaching vehicles of his pack. "Finally," he breathed. "Okay, fellahs, let's get in there and kick some ass!" With a yell, he led his fire team down the middle of the street toward the gate, firing his rifle on automatic at the remaining machine gunners. One shock trooper raised his head at an unfortunate moment and lost it, a round taking out his brain. The machine gunner opened fire, cutting down two members of C Team as Delva and two others scattered to either side of the road. Behind them, his well-protected riot car roared forward, gun ports blazing.

Missiles whistled through the air overhead, exploding inside the city. As the riot car destroyed the final resistance and smashed through the gate, another missile neared. The three motorcycles trailed after the riot car to freedom, followed by the last five members of Uncle Sam's garrison. The gate exploded, a massive fireball reaching up into the dark early morning sky.

* * *

As they approached the gate, Dusky heard the staccato popping of gunfire coupled with grenade explosions. She rode directly behind the better-armored riot car, using it for cover. Shake and Remy had pulled back to flank her. Another explosion, this one from behind them startled her. Sam clung to her, yelling into her ear.

"Missiles! From outside!"

Dusky nodded curtly. She saw Delva's fire team entering the fight before the car blocked her view. Liz and Tank began firing, Liz via a gun port and Tank with the automated firing mechanisms within the vehicle. Dusky glanced to either side, checking her backup. "Here we go!" she yelled as the car crashed through the flimsy wire barricade. They were through in seconds. Behind them, the remainder of Delva's soldiers dispatched the last of the troopers and followed on foot. It seemed almost anticlimatic.

The plan called for them to get a safe distance away and stop to pick up the soldiers. As plans are prone to do, this one went to shit. A missile skimmed by ten meters above their heads, impacting the remains of the gate. A fireball and shock wave decimated what was left of the already crumbling structure. The running soldiers and the Lichii Ba'Cho were caught on the edge of the killing field. Even at full throttle Dusky's bike jumped forward from the concussion. The riot car, with its heavier mass, wasn't as affected, and it stolidly blocked her path. Dusky fought for control, using all her strength to navigate. Sam squeezed her waist, hunkering down against her back. The back of the riot car approached fast.

Too close! No time! "Shit!" Dusky screamed. She focused her physical and spiritual being into a final act of domination and control. At the last moment, she steered the bike clear of the riot car's rear right bumper, missing it by a fraction of an inch. "Fuck me!" she crowed in relief. Her control of the bike restored, she heaved a sigh. Sam tugged frantically on her jacket, yelling at her. It was hard to hear with her ears still ringing from the explosion, but Dusky caught the words.

"We have to stop!"

Irritated, she called back, "We're still too close!" She craned her neck around to glare at Sam, her exasperation fading as she saw fear and worry. Sam's lips moved, and she made out the words "stop" and "Remy." *Remy?* Her heart in her throat, Dusky downshifted and braked, veering away from the riot car as it pulled forward without them. The tortured motorcycle roared its agony at the abrupt treatment but dutifully obeyed. She left thick black marks on the pavement as her rear tire skittered. The acrid smell of burnt rubber lent itself to the mix of incendiary smells, vehicle exhaust and smoke. The gate and apparently half of Boise was now in flames. Dusky accelerated, seeing her uncle's bike still sliding along the pavement in a crumpled heap. The flames interfered with her infrared, but her enhanced vision picked up Remy lying nearby, having just come to rest. She pulled up next to him and dived off the bike, leaving Sam to wrestle her wheels onto its kickstand.

Remy's face was covered in blood and the white of bone protruded from his unnaturally twisted left leg. Dusky felt a pulse and swallowed hard against the lump in her throat. He was unconscious, and she ran her hands over him, assessing damage. *Looks like the head and leg only. Definite concussion, blood loss.*

Sam knelt down at her side. "What do you need me to do?"

Dusky gave her a tight, grateful smile. "Hold his shoulders, pin him down. I've got to straighten this leg and set the bone back into place."

Nodding, Sam swallowed, her eyes darting over Remy's injuries. She scooted around to his head and leaned on his shoulders.

"Ready?" At Sam's nod, Dusky pulled the injured leg, working the bone back through the wound it had made. Though senseless, Remy moaned and weakly tried to move away from the pain. "Hold him!" She felt the bone grate sickeningly before she put it in place. "Okay. It's good."

Sam released Remy's shoulders as Shake pulled up on his bike. His shoulder wound had seeped through the bandages, and his eyes were wide. Dusky ripped the front of Remy's shirt off and wadded it, placing it on the leg wound and gesturing Sam closer. "Here! Put pressure on this. I don't think he severed an artery, but we have to stop the bleeding." To Shake, she ordered, "Go get Tank and Liz! We've got to get him into their car and out of here!"

Shake nodded vigorously and chased after the riot car.

Wrestling with Remy's belt, Dusky pulled it off and wrapped it around his leg above the compound fracture. She tightened the substitute tourniquet, glancing at Sam's pale face. "How you doing? You okay?"

Sam swallowed and nodded again. "Yeah, I'm okay."

The remainder of Uncle Sam's fire team trotted up. Delva immediately dropped at Remy's head. He produced an emergency first-aid kit from one of the many pouches on his belt and started tending the head wound. His last two soldiers took up positions to cover them. It seemed pointless, since all the fighting was taking place inside the wall. Sweat popped up along Dusky's skin as she took over applying pressure, the flames from the gate scorching her though they were over a hundred meters away. She noted blood running down Delva's face. "You've been hurt."

"Just a scrape. Took a short flight away from the gate and landed on a rock." He mopped blood away from Remy's face. "I'll be fine." He handed Dusky a blood stopper. "Here. Use this for now."

Nodding, she took it and tore the plastic open with her teeth. The thing looked like an overlarge sanitary napkin with long folds of gauze streaming from both ends. There was no time to be pretty about it, and she slapped the padded area directly onto Remy's blood-drenched shirt. Grabbing Sam's hand, she had her hold it in place while she wrapped the ends around his leg, tying a tight knot over the injury. "Done."

The riot car skidded to a halt. Tank dived out and threw open the back doors. Between him and Delva, they situated the still unconscious Remy inside. Delva and one of his soldiers climbed in, and Tank returned to the steering wheel. The second soldier mounted behind Shake to offer extra firepower should they be followed. The women got on Dusky's bike, and the convoy pulled away.

* * *

(For immediate distribution.)

TRAVEL ADVISORY: CENTRAL IDAHO
INTERSTATE 84 & TREASURE VALLEY
Monday, May 14, 2057

The Idaho Transportation Department, in conjunction with local and federal authorities has issued a travel advisory for the Treasure Valley. There have been reports of extreme violence perpetrated by the corporation Azteca to include heavy bombing in and around the city of Boise. Reports are scattered and evacuation may be in effect.

INTERSTATE 84 & TREASURE VALLEY
EXTREME CAUTION IS ADVISED!

Any sighting of the Azteca corporation vehicles should be reported to state and federal authorities immediately! They are driving white riot cars and vans with their logo prominently displayed. Their logo is a gold stylized Mayan jaguar on a black circle.

INTERSTATE 84 & TREASURE VALLEY
DO NOT ENGAGE!
AZTECA CORPORATION IS ARMED AND
EXTREMELY DANGEROUS!

CHAPTER TWENTY-EIGHT

Are You...
Dedicated?
Intelligent?
Technologically Proficient?
Hold a Computer Engineering Degree?
Yamaguchi, Inc. is Looking for YOU!

Position: Research Development Supervisor

Yamaguchi, Inc. is the leading developer of space habitats, satellites and the computers to run them. We have almost four million employees and assets nearing $6 billion! Our main office is in Tokyo, but we have regional offices all over the world—Washington, Miami, Paris, Madrid, Rio de Janeiro, London, Stockholm, Cairo, Honolulu—and that's just the beginning!

The **Research Development Supervisor** is responsible for overseeing various branches of our R&D department and supporting the methodology and techniques used by our researchers to reach their objectives. The Research Development Supervisor works closely with both the Research Team and the Research Development Management Staff as liaison to ensure successful execution of team goals and projects.

Responsibilities:

- Communicate with Researchers and Management and document business objectives.
- Select the most appropriate methods and techniques for research.
- Design comprehensive research plans for products in all stages of our corporate growth.
- Work with R&D Management Staff to oversee fieldwork.
- Interpret data, write reports and recommend future direction for the department.

Requirements:

- Four years in the computer engineering or space habitat industry.
- Academic and practical experience with a wide selection of R&D brands.
- Exceptional written and communication skills.
- Proficiency with multiple computer programs to include word processing, presentation software and spreadsheet applications.
- Bachelor's or advanced degree in computer engineering, mathematics, or the sciences.

If this describes YOU
Click the link below to submit your application and
résumé!

Apply Now!

* * *

Weary, Sam looked around as Dusky pulled to the side of a dark rest area. Behind them, the riot car and motorcycle growled to a halt and shut down. Soon, the only sounds were the gentle ticking and pinging of cooling engines and movement from the survivors as they stretched their legs. They'd been driving for a couple of hours, and this was a good chance to work out the kinks. The soldier on Shake's bike dismounted and stretched, his low voice making some sort of comment. Shake grinned and pulled his bike up on its stand, climbing off to join him. Liz opened the riot car, her voice full of grumbles about "old ladies" and "chamber pots." She made a beeline toward the dark building that housed the toilets, her flashlight bobbing through the night.

Sam released her hold on Dusky's waist as Dusky brought the bike onto its stand. She slid her hands up Dusky's back, running across warm leather until she reached the collar. She took hold of the heavy braid there and pulled it toward her, baring tanned skin at the juncture of Dusky's neck and shoulder. Her finger caressed there, and she leaned her forehead forward between Dusky's shoulder blades, deeply inhaling the aromas of leather and cinnamon and smoke.

Dusky sighed. "How you doing?"

The low voice sparked a frisson of pleasure. "I'm good." Despite herself, Sam yawned. "I think I need a new patch. The headache is coming back."

Nodding, Dusky got off the bike. "Go tell Shake you need one. I'm going to check on Remy."

"Okay." Sam stumbled as she climbed off the bike. She smiled reassurance. "I'm all right. Just not used to all this riding. My backside is going to have calluses before the month's up."

Dusky's face broke into a leer. "Maybe you need a massage."

Sam stepped into a warm embrace. "And you come from a long line of master masseuses?" She snuggled close, feeling more than hearing the quiet chuckle.

"Not really. But I'm eager to learn…" Dusky's hand snaked down to squeeze Sam's rear, pressing Sam's pelvis tight against her muscled thigh. Then it was gone, and Sam stood alone, watching Dusky walk away.

"I hate it when she does that." She turned toward Shake's bike and the two men speaking quietly there. "Hey, Shake. I need another 'dorph patch."

"You got it, *chica*." Shake dug in his saddlebag, coming up with the pouch of medical supplies while Sam and the soldier stared awkwardly at one another. "Take a couple, so you have them on hand."

"Thanks." Sam wondered if the stranger knew who she was. *Was he one of those looking for me at Ritzy's?* He didn't appear too interested in her beyond the standard attention all males awarded females. She walked away without speaking to him, peeling the old patch from the base of her neck and applying the new one.

The back doors of the riot car stood open, and Liz had returned to stand there. There was no sign of Dusky, and Sam frowned as she walked over. A faint smile washed away her frown as she saw Dusky sitting inside beside a conscious Remy. Tank snored in the front seat, his seat belt the only thing keeping him upright. Delva and a soldier curled nearby like a pair of hibernating bears. It looked like Delva had braced Remy's leg with a tire iron.

Dusky was conducting a cursory examination of Remy's wounds, glancing once at the sleeping men. "Guess I know who's pulling guard duty first."

Remy chuckled, hissing in pain at a particularly rough prod.

"Sorry."

"S'okay, Dusk. The endorphins are wearing off, is all."

Sam looked at the pouch in her hand. "Here. I just got these from Shake." At Dusky's questioning look, she rolled her eyes. "Yes, I've already taken one, mother." She tossed the pouch to Dusky.

As Dusky applied the endorphin patch to Remy's neck, she said, "You realize the leg is probably set wrong?" Remy nodded. "We'll get you to a ripperdoc in Tacoma, first thing. Have 'em reset it when they look at Sam's processor." She finished her examination and studied his face and the bandage there. "And maybe a plastic surgeon. Whaddya think?"

"I'm all for the ripperdoc." Remy adjusted himself with a grimace. He scooped up his canteen and uncapped it. "But let's skip the plastic surgery. Somebody once said that battle scars draw the women." Sam laughed, and he wiggled his eyebrows at her before taking a drink of water.

An audience had gathered. Shake leaned into the vehicle to grip Remy's shoulder with a relieved smile. The soldier with him stayed a respectful distance away, keeping an eye on their perimeter. Sam leaned against the doorway, arms crossed, watching them. Liz clambered into the driver's seat. Leaning on the headrest, Liz tucked white hair behind one ear. "Well? Now what?"

Dusky sobered. "Now we roust these lazy asses and put 'em on guard while the rest of us catch a nap." She rose from her seated position and kicked Delva's boot. "I want to be out of here as soon as we rest up. We're sure to see refugees coming this way soon, and I don't want to tangle with them over resources." As Delva dragged himself to wakefulness, Liz shook Tank. Dusky rudely awakened the sleeping soldier. "C'mon. Get up. You're on guard."

"Fuck that." The soldier snorted, rolling away from her. "I'm done with the service."

Dusky's eyes narrowed. "Get your ass up and on guard duty, or you'll be walking."

The soldier looked over his shoulder, cracking one eye, apparently debating whether or not he could take her in a fight. Sam nibbled her lower lip at the sudden tension. She'd seen Dusky practicing her martial arts. Did this guy have any training?

The moment was lost when Delva shoved the soldier, hard. "Watch it, Dougherty. She outranks me."

Dougherty grumbled but allowed Delva to push him out of the car and onto his feet. He and Tank moved away to take up positions on their perimeter while Delva remained at the car to keep Remy awake. Liz settled into her seat and reclined it with a happy sigh. Shake and his companion decided to crash on either side of the riot car as added security.

Sam followed Dusky back to her bike. She helped set up the sleepbag and an extra blanket in the scraggly grass nearby. Though exhausted from days without much sleep and the seemingly constant stress of the situation, she doubted she'd be able to rest. Her fears were unfounded as she settled into Dusky's arms. She was safe, protected; her eyes drifted closed and she slipped into oblivion.

* * *

"Yo, Dusk."

She groggily came awake. Three hours sleep out of forty-eight didn't cut it, and even her youthful body was beginning to feel the effects of the abuse. Opening tired eyes, she found Delva squatting nearby.

"Time to get up."

Dusky nodded in acknowledgment. Delva rose to his feet and headed back toward the riot car. The lingering smell of coffee wafted her direction as she stretched. The body draped across her inside the sleepbag mumbled a protest and tried to burrow. Dusky grunted in surprise and used her hand to block the worst of the damage from a sharp elbow. "*Preciada*. Wake up."

Sam groaned. "Don't wanna…"

Nothing short of a bomb going off was going to roust Sam. Dusky felt an evil grin cross her face. *Maybe something else will.* She rolled gently over, pinning Sam beneath her. Sam murmured, squirming to get more comfortable. Dusky eased up onto her elbows to free her hands. She graced Sam's skin with kisses, her lips blazing a trail along Sam's jaw, parallel to the slowly forming smile. At Sam's ear, Dusky traced it with her tongue and paused to give the lobe some intimate attention. Sam moved restlessly, and Dusky felt her lover's heart beat faster. She placed soft kisses on closed eyelids, smiling at the surprised flutter there. She paused, her face hovering close to Sam's, watching. There was no doubt she was awake—the heartbeat, ragged breathing and slightly parted lips attested to it. Sam moved against her sensuously. "Wake up, *preciada*."

With a sigh of partial disappointment, Sam opened her eyes. A soft smile graced her expression. "Mornin'," she mumbled. She tried to get her arms free to rub the sleep from her eyes but wasn't able. The tangled material and Dusky's body made it impossible to move. She relaxed under Dusky's gaze.

Smiling, Dusky lowered her head and rewarded Sam with a hot kiss. She reached down to knead Sam's rear, her other hand buried in golden hair. Sam moaned into her mouth as they moved against each other. After several minutes of exploring, Dusky pulled away, blood pounding through her body. Sam attempted to prolong the contact. As her struggles to free herself increased, Dusky rolled onto her back, her arm tightly pinning Sam in place against her. She pulled out of the kiss, finishing with a final nibble on Sam's full bottom lip. "You awake now?"

Sam grumbled in frustration. "Yes." A man's laughter caused her to crane her neck.

Dusky followed her gaze. The troublesome soldier— Dougherty, her mind supplied—drank coffee by the riot car. He'd obviously been watching them make out, and he leered and winked at them, making some snide comment to the group gathered there.

"Great," Sam muttered, flushing crimson and burying her head in the crook of Dusky's neck and shoulder.

"My, aren't you the shy one, *preciada*." Dusky smiled and squeezed her. "Don't worry about it. He'll either learn not to be rude or he'll be dead."

"Dead?" Sam lifted her head to study Dusky's face. "You wouldn't kill him for that, would you?"

"Well…" Dusky drawled, enjoying the flicker of honest concern. "Probably not." She snorted at Sam's relief. "He's just unaware of our ways. If he stays, he'd better wise up, though. Otherwise, he'll be hurting for certain." She glanced back at the others. The only change was Dougherty's grimace of pain as he held the back of his head and the glares from Delva and Shake. Tank, Liz and the second soldier remained prudently silent. "See?" Sam risked a quick look, and Dusky rolled to her side, releasing her. "C'mon. Coffee's on and we need to keep moving." She rose and stretched, Sam doing the same.

After folding and stashing the sleep gear, they joined the others. Delva shoved the rude soldier forward. "Dougherty wants to say something."

Dusky accepted a cup of coffee from Liz and sipped it, ignoring Dougherty.

After Delva poked his shoulder, Dougherty mumbled, "Sorry about laughing like that."

Handing Sam her cup, Dusky gave her a reassuring wink. She turned, arms across her chest, staring impassively. Long moments passed and Dougherty began to fidget, a flush of crimson rising from his open collar. He swallowed, nervous, eyes flickering to the others. When Dusky's stern gaze never wavered, he looked back, jaw set in anger. Pleased she'd gotten through, Dusky dropped her arms, allowing her stance and expression to become warmer and more inviting. "Not pleasant to be stared at, is it?"

Dougherty's anger dissipated, and he dropped his gaze in shame and confusion. He shook his head.

"In your culture you have houses, walls, doors and locks. In mine—" Dusky opened her arms to include everything around them. "In mine you have the road, wheels, maybe a tent. A camper or trailer if you're lucky. No doors to lock. No walls to hide behind." She stepped closer and offered her hand. "Apology accepted." He stared at her hand a split second before accepting it. She gave him an understanding smile, and he returned it with a vague expression of confusion. Turning away, Dusky looked everybody over. "Well, rations for breakfast and let's get going. The farther from Boise we are, the better off we'll be. We need to stay ahead of the refugees or we'll never get gas." She took her coffee back from Sam, wrapping an arm around Sam's waist.

After a nutritious meal of military rations, they prepared to leave. The grayness of dawn had made way for blue skies. Dark trees became less shadow and more scraggly growth. The rest area had become home to several other vehicles during their nap. An unspoken truce had sprung up among the refugees, a peace of sorts no doubt facilitated by the number of automatic weapons on hand. Delva took Shake's bike with the other soldier, Correa, riding pillion. Dougherty rode shotgun in the riot car with Tank driving. Liz and Shake remained in the back of the riot car with Remy.

As Dusky kicked her bike over, the sky brightened behind her. The illumination was so sudden and strong it looked like midday except that the shadows were too long and faced the wrong direction. Several refugees turned and stared, some in shock, others exclaiming in anger and fear. Dusky turned to see the fading flash and the top of a mushroom cloud rising in the desert. It was small but enough to trigger a wave of terror. "Let's get out of here." She helped Sam onto the bike behind her. The Lichii Ba'Cho left the rest area, the first of a mass exodus of people fleeing the tactical nuclear missile that had been unleashed on the once great city of Boise, Idaho.

* * *

Sam's backside had long stopped hurting. It felt as numb as she did. She vaguely toyed with the idea of going through life with a petrified butt, wondering if she'd ever be able to walk again. Her lower back made up for the lack of sensation. It was on fire. She tried to ease the ache by stretching in place. It didn't do much good. When Dusky finally slowed, Sam was groggily surprised. Once again in forested mountains, they threaded down a long abandoned logging road on the far side of Couer d'Alene. A clearing opened on the right, and Dusky pulled into it. When she shut off the bike, Sam almost missed the vibration beneath her. The riot car and other bike shut down, leaving the clearing in the first silence Sam had heard in eight hours. She made a half-hearted attempt to stand, but her thighs argued against that proposal. Dusky's help was the only way Sam was able to dismount. She stood in creaky pain as Dusky put the bike on its stand and grudgingly slid off the bike. Sam felt a moment's pleasure that she wasn't the only one suffering.

"We'll stay here the night, but keep close and keep your heads up." Dusky winced as she dug her fingers into the small of her back. "Last week we had some trouble in this area. I can't guarantee someone didn't call the sheriff when we went by."

Delva grunted, rubbing his face. "You sure you got 'em all?"

All what? Sam frowned, her sluggish mind taking time to make the connections.

Dusky nodded. "Sorry, output. The Aryans have been hunted out of this area. We'll have to try somewhere else."

He snorted, a scowl on his face. "Too bad."

Sam blinked, her wary eyes darting around the clearing in search of racist good ol' boys looking for a fight.

Tank exited the riot car, coming around to open the back. Dougherty jumped down from the passenger seat. "Why'd we stop here?"

"Because some of us are exhausted." Correa slung his rifle across his shoulders and twisted back and forth to work the kinks out of his muscles.

Dusky didn't quite hobble, at least not as much as Sam did as they walked to the car and opened one rear door. Remy looked more comfortable than last time as he lounged on a collection of packs and blankets. "How are you doing, Uncle?"

Remy's expression was wry. "Better than you." He peered out the door and windows, craning his neck. "This where we're supposed to meet them?"

Sam followed his gaze, seeing nothing but sickly trees and brush. *No Aryans.* "Meet who?"

"Yeah." Dusky stretched her arms high over her head. "We had plans to meet with the Pacific Federated Tribes here. We were headed to cancel the meeting when we came across you. I'm actually surprised they aren't here already." She looked away from Sam, regarding the others. "We'll pack it in for the night. Dougherty, Tank and Liz have first watch." Dusky spoke over Dougherty's groan, ignoring his whinge. "Like I said, we had trouble here last week. Maybe the shit storm in Boise overshadowed it, but we're wanted in this county. Keep your eyes sharp."

They got to work preparing a campsite. Sam pondered their forced road trip as she cleared an old firepit and collected wood. The trip north had been in reverse order for her. They'd roared north along the highway, surrounded by scraggly forest, following the river into the mountains, sharing the road with other displaced people fleeing for their lives. Abandoned personal belongings and vehicles had littered the shoulders of the state highway. Sam thought she'd seen dead bodies in some places, the victims of looting left to rot in the warm spring morning. There'd been no rest stops as the Lichii Ba'Cho made way at top speed, no layovers to stretch their legs, ignoring any resistance raised by the townships they passed through and around.

A blockade had been set up at Horseshoe Bend. City police and deputized citizens stood on the wall, weapons ready as the officials argued with a crowd of a couple of hundred demanding entry at the southern gate. Dusky hadn't paused there, leading her people along the pedestrian path to the left, passing through the now abandoned shantytown. Not even the dogs had remained behind. Sam had seen soldiers and farmers with guns positioned on the walls, watching as the vehicles skirted the city. Hitting the road on the other side, the pack had bypassed another explosive argument in the making at the north gate. As they'd sped away Sam had heard gunfire and had peered backward to see the mass of people boiling at the base of the gate. She'd cringed away, thinking the world was coming to an end.

The same scenes had played along the lower state highway corridor. Thousands of Boise residents had fled at the initial Azteca attack more than twenty-four hours before, blazing a trail of derelict automobiles and forsaken possessions that the Lichii Ba'Cho and the new rush of exiles followed, breadcrumbs of despair leading to no safe haven. Smaller townships had suffered much worse than the walled cities. The city of Banks was a hulking ruin, fire having razed it to the ground. As the Lichii Ba'Cho drove through, Sam saw desolate residents poking among the still smoking buildings and at least three bodies hanging from a tree in the town's central square.

Through the mountains, the landscape had opened up, revealing a wide valley of farmland and small communities untouched by the chaos behind them. They'd made it ahead of most the refugees by that point. One gas station in Grangeville agreed to sell them enough fuel to fill the riot car's tank, and they topped off the bikes at another. Sam had hoped they'd stop longer, but instead Dusky pressed on through Cottonwood and Ferdinand. They had eventually passed the walled city of Lewiston. The scene there had been much different than the one in Horseshoe Bend. No crowd demanded entry, and the gates stood open though manned by police in riot gear. Smoke had smudged the sky above, indicating the havoc inside triggered by the virus. Refugees might not have reached that far, but the power outage had created its own chaos.

Furtive movement brought Sam back to the present. She blinked, peering into the undergrowth, brow furrowed. *A squirrel?* Nothing moved and she wondered if she'd imagined it. She stood, looking around the clearing for the others. She saw Dougherty and Correa down by the water with buckets. Liz and Tank puttered around their vehicle, rooting through their belongings. Dusky, Shake and Delva had disappeared. Remy, tucked back in the riot car, held his finger to his lips when Sam's gaze met his. He twitched his hand, indicating Sam should join him.

She swallowed in sudden fear, heart racing as she complied. Her back was ramrod stiff, and it was all she could do not to turn her head to look for the danger. Off to her left, she saw more movement from the corner of her eye and quickened her pace. At the car, she forced herself to smile. "How are you doing, Remy?" Now she saw he wore his radio headset, the one that connected with Dusky and Shake.

"Fantastic, *señorita*. But I could use another 'dorph patch." He patted the floorboard beside him. "I can't reach them, though. Can you get it for me?"

"Sure." Liz peered solemnly at her over the back of the passenger seat. Sam crawled in, hearing something drop on the ground at Tank's position and the large man scrabbling on the ground.

"Close the doors."

Sam gave a bare nod at Remy's whisper. "Oh, here's the first-aid kit." She darted forward, grabbing the door handle and slamming it shut. At the same time, Liz did the same, scrambling to the driver's seat where she locked and loaded the turret-mounted weapons. There was a bump along the bottom of the riot car, indicating that Tank had taken up position beneath them. "What is it? What's out there?"

Remy shook his head, wincing as he scooted toward the front to get a better view of the weapons screen. "Don't know. Could be our friends. Could be the law."

Peeking out the back window, Sam scanned the clearing. From this angle she couldn't see the soldiers collecting water. She chewed her lower lip, hoping Dusky's disappearance was the result of going to ground rather than being arrested or attacked.

"I've got dozens of targets on IR." Liz panned the turret cam around the clearing. "Too damned quiet for cops. It had better be your people."

"Where's Dusky?" Sam looked over her shoulder at Remy. "I know you're on the radio. Is she okay?"

Remy held up a hand. "She's fine, *señorita*. Quiet, please." He spoke into the microphone in a mixture of Spanish and English, relaying Liz's information to the Lichii Ba'Cho still outside.

Sam stared out the window. She sensed more than saw movement to one side and heard Correa swear. The sound of water sloshing to the ground accompanied Liz's report.

"They've got Dougherty and Correa. Those aren't proper uniforms—it's not the authorities out there."

The thought that the Aryans had regrouped terrified Sam. She scrambled to the front to catch sight of what Remy was now describing to Dusky on the radio. Dougherty was out cold on the ground. Correa sat cross-legged beside him, hands behind his back and a gag being tied off in his mouth by a no-nonsense looking man in brown leather. The stranger had three friends with him, casually holding weapons as they

210 D Jordan Redhawk

surrounded their prisoners. As he finished tying the gag, he stood, and Sam realized he was Native American. "Wait. Isn't that one of the people you're waiting for?"

Liz tapped a control on the dashboard, zeroing in on the man as he glared back at the camera. "Tank, don't shoot. You copy?" From under them, they felt a knock. Liz pulled back the camera view once again, panning quickly around to show other Indians emerging from their hiding places. She turned to look at Remy. "What now?"

In answer, Dusky appeared on the screen, hands out and open. She approached the apparent leader, the one holding Dougherty and Correa. Sam swallowed hard, forcing away the sting of relieved tears. *Not now!* She watched Dusky speak, not able to hear her words. They conversed back and forth a tense moment. Something was said, and the three companions of the newcomer brought their weapons to bear. Before they could do more, Delva and Shake materialized from behind them. Shake disarmed one, and Delva simply slammed the two others together hard enough to drop them in their tracks. Sam fought the desire to close her eyes, refusing to cringe away from the inevitable destruction of Dusky.

The newcomer smirked, making some comment to the disgraced warriors at his feet. He held up his hand. "Hold your fire! We're among friends."

Sam's breath hitched in her chest as she inhaled. Dusky closed the distance, reaching out to shake the man's hand. She turned and looked at the riot car. "Stand down!" Sam sagged in relief. Liz shut down the weapons console, opening the door to help Tank wriggle out from beneath the vehicle and stand.

Sam felt a hand on her shoulder and saw Remy's kind smile, tentatively returning it. She climbed forward, exiting through the passenger door. She had to touch Dusky, to assure herself that all was well. One of the strangers had begun untying Correa while Shake and another attempted to wake Dougherty. Sam bypassed them, not caring if she was screwing up any cultural norm among the American Indian people as she slid into Dusky's arms. Apparently no insult was taken as the man smiled at her.

"Sam Elias, this is Jackson Dokibahl from the Pacific Federated Tribes. He's here to help."

CHAPTER TWENTY-NINE

(Excerpt, British Columbia Press-Tribune, dated Monday, 5/14/2057)

According to the Canadian Government Ministry today, any country willing to sign a nonaggression pact with Canada and its allied nations will receive much- needed aid in dealing with the so-called Courier Virus. Additionally, the pact will assist those countries with skilled and non-skilled labor to bring them out of the twenty-first century dark ages that they have fallen into. Spokesman Robert Bremerton states, "What has happened in the United States is a tragedy of the highest magnitude. It can easily be diverted. We were fortunate enough to be able to defeat the virus in our country, and look forward to sharing that information with others. All we want is to live in a peaceful world with our neighbors."

* * *

<u>(Excerpt, Azteca Regional Newsletter, dated week of August 23, 2057)</u>

TRANSFERS AND PROMOTIONS!!
Congratulations to two lucky individuals this month!

First, KENNETH SHIMIZU has made the grade! He's transferring to our primary office in South Dakota to continue his work and dedication as the Midwest Regional Security Director. Ken has been with our company for twenty-two years and has an exemplary record. We were unable to get hold of Ken for a few words, but wish him the best. Good one, Ken!

Replacing him will be TED HARRELSON, formerly Ken's assistant. Ted's been working with Azteca for nine years, and this is a major step up for him. "I'm looking forward to the challenge," he said. "Getting our systems virus-free and back online is one of my top priorities." When asked about the rumors that have been floating around the Hermiston Corporate office: "The allegations that Mr. Shimizu was forced to commit ritual suicide (seppuku) on his employer's office floor are greatly exaggerated. Ken's a great man and a good friend. I wish him all the best in the future."

* * *

While the traditional field was nowhere near as full as she remembered from her youth, Dusky felt proud of the thirty-plus survivors and recruits scattered before her. She stood on a slight rise, surveying her people as they went about their new lives. Vehicles, campers and a few tents filled the bowl-shaped field. Liz and Tank had set up shop in a midsized motorhome, having gutted the interior to build a mobile tech shop. Right now, Tank fiddled with a collapsible satellite dish while Liz yelled directions from inside as they searched for a viable satellite net connection.

Remy lounged in a cracked plastic lawn chair before his tent, the cast on his leg no longer the pristine white it had once been. A small fire kept a pot of coffee warm, and three wide-eyed children sat at his feet listening to him spin a yarn. Considering the nature of his injury, the cast would remain on for another couple of months, and he'd have trouble walking for the rest of his life. That hadn't fazed him—he'd already picked up a secondhand three-wheel motorcycle that he towed behind Delva's riot car, waiting for the day he could ride again. The long, deep facial scar was a permanent fixture, giving him the dangerous look he had craved. Despite the setbacks, he was healing well.

Dusky's eyes wandered over the children. Two held the telltale features and coloring of American Indians. The third boasted white-blond hair and blue eyes—Al Dougherty's son. The others belonged to the handful of Pacific Tribe members that had wanted to come on the road with the Lichii Ba'Cho.

The Pacific Federated Tribes had been very generous with their aid, giving Dusky and her ragtag group of refugees everything they had needed to replenish their losses. After two weeks of waiting for Remy to be declared able to travel, four families and two extra warriors had joined their ranks. One of them was a medicine man trained in the rituals and magic of his people. Richard was of an age with Remy, and the two elders spent hours warming their bones by the fire, reminiscing of the Before-Time of the golden twentieth century. He supplied the nomads with much-needed spiritual guidance, counsel that Dusky hadn't realized she had missed until it presented itself again.

At the center of the field stood a tall pole with six ropes dangling from above. Painted red, its top was decorated with bone and clay fetishes that clicked against the wood in the summer breeze. A beaten path circled it, darkened in places where blood had spilled. Shake had conducted himself well during the Sun Dance. He'd lasted longer than Dougherty or Correa had. *That's to be expected; they weren't raised in our ways.* It had surprised her when Dougherty had decided to stay. She'd expected him to bolt as soon as they'd arrived in Couer d'Alene. Instead, he'd contacted his wife and had her come out to meet them in Seattle. She recalled his green complexion as Delva explained the mechanics of the Sun Dance to him. Still, Dougherty had toughed it out surprisingly well and had seemed to settle more within himself.

Dusky inhaled deeply, smelling roasting meat from the cook fires. The Sun Dance complete, the clan would celebrate with a feast. There'd be drums and dancing and alcohol and laughter. Richard had a ceremony ready for the next day to commemorate the spirits of their dead. After the hellacious May they'd had, it was a welcome relief to find something to celebrate.

She felt a presence behind her and smiled, not turning. Seconds later, arms wrapped around her waist and she felt Sam's chin rest on her shoulder as their bodies molded together. Dusky rested her arm on top of the one at her waist, wrapping their light and dark fingers together. "*Preciada.*"

"Hi." Sam gave Dusky a slight squeeze before moving to stand beside her. She smiled. "Shake's doing good. Just finished the stitches and Richard's starting the tat."

Dusky turned, gathering Sam into her arms. "And how are you?" She gently thumbed the four small feather tattoos decorating Sam's face.

Sam winced a little at the contact. "They feel bruised, but that's all." She grinned. "Actually, I kind of like them." Her face screwed into a scowl. "Makes me look wild and dangerous, don't you think?" She grinned ruefully at the responding laughter, slapping Dusky's arm. "Hey! You saying I don't look dangerous?"

Laughing aloud, Dusky held Sam tight. "No, no! I'd never say that!" Her chuckles faded into a wide smile. "You're very dangerous, *preciada*. You have my heart."

"And you have mine." Sam murmured back.

Dusky enjoyed the sense of warmth and security that always filled her when Sam was in her arms. No one had ever made her feel this way before, and she had no plans to ever let Sam go. They stood quietly, wrapped in each other until Sam's stomach rumbled. Dusky snickered. "C'mon, let's get you fed." She released Sam. "We don't want you fainting away from hunger tonight...Too much partying to do."

Sam's blush subsided and she grinned. "Partying, eh? I think I'm going to like being Lichii Ba'Cho." They walked toward their family, arm in arm.

* * *

(Excerpt, Washington Post, dated April 9, 2058)

In a bold move today, Congress indicted General Daniel C. McAndrews on several charges of war crimes that were committed in the Boise Massacre last summer.

"The man had no right bringing tactical nukes into the fight," said Senator Jimmie Allar of Washington (Rep.) "There's nothing left but a sunken hole in the ground! The half-life alone is going to keep people from living anywhere in the Treasure Valley for the next three thousand years!"

Neither Gen. McAndrews or his attorney, Daniel Cunningham, were available for comment.

Bella Books, Inc.

Women. Books. Even Better Together.

P.O. Box 10543
Tallahassee, FL 32302

Phone: 800-729-4992
www.bellabooks.com